T0193200

THE BIG THOUGHT
READING MACHINE

THE BIG THOUGHT READING MACHINE

FICTION OR NOT, THIS IS WHAT I GOT

Gianina Sipitca

Copyright © 2019 by Gianina Sipitca.

| ISBN: | Softcover | 978-1-7960-1925-4 |
| | eBook | 978-1-7960-1924-7 |

All rights reserved. No part of this book may be reproduced or transmitted in any form or by any means, electronic or mechanical, including photocopying, recording, or by any information storage and retrieval system, without permission in writing from the copyright owner.

This is a work of fiction. Names, characters, places and incidents either are the product of the author's imagination or are used fictitiously, and any resemblance to any actual persons, living or dead, events, or locales is entirely coincidental.

Any people depicted in stock imagery provided by Getty Images are models, and such images are being used for illustrative purposes only.
Certain stock imagery © Getty Images.

Print information available on the last page.

Rev. date: 03/07/2019

To order additional copies of this book, contact:
Xlibris
1-888-795-4274
www.Xlibris.com
Orders@Xlibris.com
604033

CONTENTS

DEDICATION

To those who push the limits, to those who constantly wish to expand the horizon, in order to be happier more complete human beings inside this circle of life, planet Earth.

PROLOGUE

A Thought Reading Machine linked to the DNA of the Anchor means Complete Loss of Privacy yet can help protect those whose spirit and body is taken over by Goulds.

In Fiction Or Not, This Is What I Got (The Big Thought Reading Machine) a jealousy driven first lady Hillary Obama, paranoid presidential hopeful Michelle Clinton, meet playboy billionaire Mikhail Prokhorov in new modern day America, SciFi novel about fictional character the Tsarina, with an IQ of 7000, who is told that she is a messenger of God and has to marry her husband to be, the real life billionaire. She has subliminal conversations about how to save the world one person at a time, from the Goulds, leprosy and the complete loss of privacy with evil politicians and superior minded business moguls.

The novel starts with an introspect look at her life, by Dulkinna, the main character, who, while working on an autobiographic novel and periodically writing poems in her notebook, reminisces about her first becoming acutely aware about the fact that she really, really is the center of everybody's attention. It inserts as in a time capsule returned from the future, the poems Dulkinna wrote during the game and some of her own writings for the novel.

Later, the author defines the awareness of the Big Thought Reading Machine, the ripe marriage of Dulkinna and Ioobe and Dulkinna is branded as paranoid. When she vows to never let them destroy her conscience she starts hearing the voices of the system.

The Chapter What Do These People Want From Us, is about Dulkinna's incipient politically charged discussions with the Dalai Lama or the President of America, at the same time the Big Thought Reading Machine becomes more and more advanced and described maybe in deeper detail, as far as Dulkinna intuitively understands it.

The Thanks Giving Trip to Las Vegas chapter, introduces Mikhail Prokhorov, the real life playboy billionaire and Russian presidential candidate that eventually steals Dulkinna's heart and starts the subliminal dialogs. Dulkinna Googles her subliminal lover, the only one she is not afraid to make love at subliminal level with, even on the machine. She becomes hopelessly in love with this second man and recognizes his cooing on the machine.

Dulkinna and Mikhail Prokhorov start talking about their 250 children. Most of the rest of the novel is a continuous subliminal dialogue between Dulkinna and the haters or other players of the Game.

The Chapter: What, How, Where Went Wrong? is about the actual suicide. After a clinical death, for two and a half days, Dulkinna wakes up and immediately writes some poems during a group session.

CHAPTER ONE

I remember Him With Every Christmas

I was born and raised in communist Romania. I had a younger brother, Linu and many uncles, aunts and cousins. I would say I had a large family, in which I grew up, was educated loved and taken care of, by almost every other member of the family. Almost every one of my relatives, from elders to the younger ones, taught me something. I now live in the United States with my husband and try to keep in touch with those who are scattered throughout Europe, or I remember the loved departed ones. The most beloved ones that I lost, were my maternal grandmother, who helped raise me and my younger brother Linu. We lived only five minutes from our grandmother's house. She was the true matron. Her word of advice was sought after, by everybody I remember, inside and outside our family. She was the one who took charge of the spiritual education of my brother and I, in a country where practicing ones religion was forbidden by the communist party and where religious expression was frowned upon outside close circles of friends and family. People were afraid. One could have started a religious conversation, only to entrap another and report them to the secret services. One could create a lot of problems and unpleasant issue for somebody, that way.

My grandmother did not preach to us much. She taught us that God is omnipresent and that we should not worry that the communists did not want us to go to church. She said that He knows everything and knows we should not endanger ourselves or our family, but that we should live our lives in the way God intended. The main tenet was to "not do unto others what you do not like to have done onto yourself". I remember her saying that He knows the way we think and it is not of use to try and be hypocritical. We had to love and respect Him and His will. It was not very hard for us to understand her simple words and the fact that it was to be our secret, made it all the more powerful in our little innocent hearts.

For my brother and I, religion, at the time, meant praying from time to time, when we were supervised, always when we were scared of something and knowing that you can never lie to God almighty. We always crossed ourselves when passing by the church, even in front of everybody else, we confessed and took communion for Easter and Christmas only. Easter and Christmas were always celebrated in the family and of course, my grandmother was the big matron, who directed or was otherwise implicated in every aspect. These holydays, we always were in the family. We never skipped them.

We always tried to go to church for Easter, but usually in a different town from ours, where we would not be well known. For us, the children, it was an opportunity to take a short vacation, we were always dressed in nice new clothes and loved seeing the new places and eat the good food. At Christmas, it was even more fun. We always had to be at our own home and we would receive a visit from Santa Clause. Usually, for each little present, we would have to answer a few questions, after which we had to entertain Santa with a poem or a short caroling. We were always eager with anticipation and my parents, grandmother and aunts and uncles, were always preparing us, by asking: "Do you know what to tell Santa this year? remember, he already knows everything". I guess, for us, this cemented that belief that there is somebody out there WHO KNOWS!

One year, for the Easter confession, our grandmother took us directly to school, in our brand new clothes, without our uniforms, saying that the priest had blessed our attire and we should not change that day. Once there, every one of our classmates was asking why do we not wear our required uniforms? The teachers, to whom the grandmother talked to, were silent. However, the school principal, put a call for our father to be allowed from his job to come to school immediately.

My little brother was bragging to everybody, that he had taken communion and that he is wearing his blessed new clothes that our mother had bought for Easter. Once there, my father "blamed" the mother in law. I later found that they had an understanding. He claimed, that "one cannot taken the old ones out of their ingrained old preconceptions about the existence of God and that since the grandmother was taking care of us, we had been contaminated, sort of speak". The principal was an old fox and he told my father, that he is to make sure we do not propagate these misbeliefs and to make sure we know the truth. In the next couple of days, our grandmother gently informed us that we should never be as impolite as to claim that our teachers were lying to us, since, God already knows, that it is the communists who make all of us say, but only in school are we allowed to say, that there is no supernatural power. She told us that in general, we should keep our beliefs to ourselves, never be untrue and always know that He knows the reason for everything.

On another occasion, the leader of the communist party, Toader Ceausescu was coming to visit our town. In classes, we were being prepared for answering questions from the principal who was looking for a little boy and girl to offer him flowers. In my brother's kindergarten class, the teacher asked the children if they knew who was the all-powerful over all Romania. My little brother, raised his little hand, started waiving it and never took no for an answer. He wanted to be the one to give the answer. The teacher, somewhat reluctantly asked: "Ok, Linu, who do you think it is?" "God almighty" came the answer. "He is the only one all-powerful over every one of us". The teacher told him that he was mistaken, that in Romania, it was comrade Ceausescu and that he had not paid attention in class.

Then, the next day, the teacher asked the question again. My brother's class was posed the same question, in front of the principal. My little brother, raised his hand, waiving happily. The teacher's heart had shrunk. She froze. Then, my brother, started talking: "comrade teacher, please allow me to give the answer, I promise, I will say Ceausescu and I will never say that God almighty is the All-powerful One in school again". My father had to be brought to order again..

In the beginning of summer of 1989, just before the anticommunist revolution of December, I had lost my little brother, who had just celebrated his twentieth birthday, six days before. I thought that the earth should open and swallow me whole. We had loved each other dearly. He had been my best friend and my biggest fan. I kept thinking during the funeral, that God cannot allow such thing. I will grow old and Linu would not. I will see the world over and would not have my younger brother to send postcards to. But most of all, it is hard at Christmas. When we celebrate the birth of the Lord, I remember the big fir trees my father used to buy, our lighting it with anticipation and waiting for Santa. Of course, Santa had stopped coming to us, but in my parents' house, he sometimes paid visits for our little cousins or even neighbor's children. Christmas is not the same without my precocious, endearing brother. After all this time, I still remember him, his naughty little misbehaviors and his trying to wear a cross on a chain around his neck, even in the communist military school where he was killed.

If I could become hatred itself,
His disdain to show you for your lies,
If I could hatred to show you, flesh and bones,
To make you see it's gaze,
To make you know it's liking.
Now, after your despicable deeds,
Do not seek my forgiveness,
It will look just like Him.
But you will recognize it,
Without seeing His blue eyes.
You will want to yawn.
Without hearing His sweet voice,
You will want to go to sleep.
You will know what you did wrong and when.

You will recognize your despicable thought
And dieing you will rot.
For you, ugly, wandering soul,
I pray!

If I could become warmth itself,
If I could show you how much lack of hatred,
How much kindness in His advice,
How much sweetness in His childhood voice.
He was endearing, naughty and had a big heart
He was looking for love and attention,
If not, he was eager to give it to you,
Without too much ado.
This is how he used to love,
My little brother,
He used to always amaze me
With His celestial mind.
He was the one advising,
That I should be doing my thing,
He was surrounding my being,
Only with those without hatred.
He was asking for advice,
Only to prove I was wise.
To show me sweetness and tell me
That he was proud of his big sister,
Whom he always introduced with reverence.

I was for Him, a curse on this earth,
He was for me, the most sacred word.
I was for Him, the horrible sister,
Who never asked:
Are you in pain? Do you encounter disdain?
Can I help?
I thought if I cared was enough,
I thought I was supposed to be too tough!

How would I know, I would push them,
To the wretchedness of extinguishing you?

My Morning Star they wanted you to be,
We kept believing we are but two children.

At the end, in your last gaze,
You did not want to let me know!
Your gaze was still warmth, you were still believing,
That it is still good, for me to be here and you there, somewhere.

CHAPTER TWO

Big Thought Reading Machine

For centuries, trained people could read each other's minds, influence each other's decisions, give each other feelings of love, hatred or envy. It was only for "superior individuals" though to "participate" in "the game". The "Stupids" were to be prayed upon, their individual intelligence tapped into by the initiated. Now, in the 21st Century, the Big Thought Reading Machine invention allowed "stupids" to defend themselves from the superiors and at the same time pray on each other. The machine, together with the system, can give you an orgasm, make you vote republican, ask you subliminal questions, tap into your creative intelligence and when you are inconvenient in any way, it can easily, untraceably kill you.

The Electorate

Is mind control really a thing?
Can something like this be happening?
Of course it can, but of course it should not,
Mean that it happens a lot.
He wants my 10 dollars,
But not my 2 cents,
I'll give him the later,
Without pretense.

Dulkinna, the "lab rat" used by the machine to collectively tap into her nervous system, was dabbed "the cow". She was a cash cow for the system and the corporations. But most of all, her owner, the father of the games. A superior individual, Dulkinna had never been trained at subliminal level, out of fears she would easily become better than any other superior. This enhanced her creativity and value in the business world. Rather than tap into other people intelligence, Dulkinna was always using her own resources during her favorite pass time, problem solving.

She was passionate about a number of subjects: from politics to science, literature, social sciences and cooking. But most of all, they loved using her kid like charm so that the libido enhancing capabilities of the machine could be marketed. The machine glitch made it such that every woman envied, hated and wanted to be her and every man mistakenly thought he was in love with the cow.

The women started the "Conference for the women" where they discussed how to kill the cow. The stupid hatred and envy became so big that the first lady herself came with a plan for destroying "that bitch". She learned everything about the human metabolism under the pretext of the child obesity. She now knew how to make Dulkinna artificially gain weight while eating strawberries. If she had a little bit of soup with some fat in it, the first lady and her system of "queens of Sheeba" could make Dulkinna gain a couple of pounds within the hour.

Many could not imagine that their thoughts were open to others to see. Continuously they were flabbergasted by their fears, into playing the game and pretending that only Dulkinna's nervous system can be used by the machine and that, led Dulkinna into reaching the conclusion that continuous war and insanity would follow.

They were so busy amusing themselves with making her gain weight or altering her appearance, or with giving themselves multiple orgasms with the machine that used her nervous system, that she was unsuccessful in bringing their attention to the dangers that the machine was posing for their own lives and livelihood even.

She was considered so superior that society decided to harvest her eggs and they had approximately 250 living children of Dulkinna, born by surrogates who wanted either to have a superior child in the family, or to raise one of them for body parts. The children born from her DNA were always the most devoted individuals, who gave their lives gladly for their parents or for a just and righteous cause. Just like Dulkinna's brother had done years before.

He was a trained superior, who had allowed himself to be killed in a ritualistic fashion, in order to prevent the murder of his untrained elder sister or that of her husband. The governments who "owned" the game, wanted to bring a tragedy into her life, to see how would she develop socially. They called it building "the cow's" character.

Started as a joke, they decided to kill him the way the great Roman emperor Caesar had been killed. His own friends and some family members participated in the crime, for the sake of which, everybody betrayed the fine young man. The governments and the Council were satisfied, but they could not explain why. A feeling of guilt ensued and every participant embarked on the new endeavor of covering their tracks and blaming those who suffered the most, namely Dulkinna and her husband, for the killing.

He had been the most warm, loving and caring individual that Dulkinna has ever known. Since he was baby, in his mother's arms, he used to follow and pay close attention to his big sister and signal how much he would love her. There was no sibling rivalry? Yes, it was, but the brotherly love between them surmounted all obstacles. It was as if God All Mighty took the time to be with Him on this Earth, to guide His every move and deed, to calm and warm His Heart and Thought. The fire in His turquoise Eyes would be the Force that will guide Dulkinna throughout the rest of her life, to show her what was good and where there was evil. He came to know that, during His short time of parting His wisdom to her and took care to great length that Dulkinna remembers both at over-liminal and at subliminal level that force. That had become her guiding Light, her Shining Morning Star. 23 years after his murder, Dulkinna wrote a poem about Him and the Big Thought Reading Machine and the game: If I Could….

CHAPTER THREE

The Grandiose Wedding Reception

We all have a place in ourselves, where we think our thoughts are formed, where we think the feelings come from, I used to call it "that place in my heart". Where everything starts taking shape, where I kept the memory of my little brother, of the little girl that I used to be and where I placed Ioobe carefully a couple of days before our civil ceremony, in a secret vow I made in front of God.

I was having diner in a night club in Bucharest with one of my former beaus and in the middle of the conversation, in which we were basically saying good bye and chatting about my coming nuptials, I had a thought that kept forming and gently came to the surface, giving me a shiver down my spine.

I detached from the conversation and decided to be with the thought, to make a vow, right then, to myself and God, that I will cherish and obey my new husband, that I will love him till the end of my life and that this will be my secret wish and driving force in life. I decided then, that I would never stop trying to understand him, to fight for our marriage and most of all for his happiness. It just came to me as a conclusion, that my happiness will follow from all this. That the happier I will try and make my husband, the happier I will be, the more love I will impart to him, the more love I will feel in my life.

Ioobe and I were finishing our studies in electrical engineering and we decided that we should start our new life as engineers, hand in hand, by getting married and living life to its fullest, together. We both agreed on this, we both felt it was the right thing and natural next step even though, in those days, we did not always see everything eye to eye. We did, however, both realize that we have something special together.

He had a natural inclination to try and take care of my every need, while I was always obsessed about being a veritable partner in life, of contributing my share to our family life, even though I had this tendency to not let show everything. I was even told from time to time, that I might be the kind of person who just takes and takes and never gives.

It was one of the most hurtful things my friends could tease me with. Not only did I like to give myself in every way; I always felt the need to be generous as a daughter, as a friend, as a sister, a granddaughter and niece, a lover. When making love to Ioobe, I always wondered if I am a good lover, I wished sometimes to switch places, to feel his feelings, to be able to judge my love making act, was it giving him the most wonderful of feelings, was the experience as good as I wanted it to be? I am not sure I wanted him to give me good marks, I wanted to give them to myself.

My fiance© always seemed to say, "you are the one for me", without giving me too many lines, it was always deeper, with every one of his deeds, with his entire attitude, with every fiber of his being. Yet, I wanted to doubt it, I wanted to never take it for granted, I wanted to wonder: "do I make him completely happy"? Will I know when he is hurting, will I always be there, will it be hard or easy, will I always take pleasure in anticipating his every need?

We were not necessarily finishing each other sentences. In fact, the bed was the only place where he never criticized me, where he gave me compliment after compliment and where we seemed to make music those days. Not having a place of our own in the beginning had been the sweetest of set ups for our hot romance. I shared a room with three other girls and sneaking into bed when everybody wanted to go see a good movie, skipping classes when we could have the room to ourselves or not going to a party in order to stay in, this is how we spiced up our romance. We went to parties, movies, theater plays, restaurants and bars, more than any of my friends, yet, I remember giving many of them up if we really could have the room just for us.

We had our civil ceremony only with close friends. We had the best dancing party and any one I know still remembers it as such. Probably due to the cognac; It was the highlight of the evening. Everything was good, food, wine, beer, but the cognac was a special order that my father had placed directly with a producer. I was not much of a drinker, but we kept getting compliment after compliment for it and everybody, one after another, "fell victim" to its qualities, as if drinking from an elixir. It was our special party. Everybody already envied our love story and our luck for having found each other.

On the day of the wedding, I had a reality check. It was one of the biggest wedding parties I ever partook in. People were coming, telling me that even though I do not know them, they know me very well and that they would very much love to wish me good luck and happiness in our marriage and if it was at all possible, they would have liked to party with us. The restaurant eventually ran out of chairs and tables and people just told us it was OK. They did not need to sit down. Just to be with us for a couple of hours. The downside of the evening was when my brother Linu came to tell me that they ran out of Pepsi. They did not bring him any at the table, told him they ran out and he was worried about the other guests. I did not care. All I could think of was what I told the waitress: "THIS IS THE BROTHER OF THE BRIDE. HE WILL HAVE HIS DRINK. WHERE IS HIS PEPSI?" He got scared. Started calming me down, while the waitress promised to go to an adjacent restaurant to procure some. There were so many people present, that about two weeks after, I met a very close friend and told her: "Too bad you could not come to the wedding, it was such fun". She was perplexed: "But Dulkinna, I was there, we had a conversation together, she said watching the expression on my face change into stupor and adding, you were so busy entertaining so many guests, no wonder you forgot."

At the time I did not pay too much attention to how many people knew me, even though I did not know them. I kept telling myself that it is because of my parents, grandmother or uncle being so well known. However, I was always aware of it. I used to walk down the street and notice people taking stock of my appearance, noticing whom I was with and so on. I was living in a small city, not exactly a town and even though everybody knew me, I could not know who everybody was. I knew though that they knew me. Still, what happened at the wedding was a surprise. I had never heard of such a thing. Of so many people coming uninvited to bring a gift and congratulate the new couple. It seemed to be the announcing of a prosperous and happy marriage and every one in my family remembers the whole year, as being one of the most happy ones in our lives.

One year after the wedding, my father in law had died, my brother had been killed in the military school he was attending. He had been the most warm, loving and caring individual that I have ever known. Since he was baby, in his mother's arms, he used to follow and pay close attention to his big sister and signal how much he would love her. There was no sibling rivalry? Yes, it was, but the brotherly love between us surmounted all obstacles. It was as if God All Mighty took the time to be with Him on this Earth, to guide His every move and deed, to calm and warm His Heart and Thought. The fire in His turquoise Eyes would be the Force that will guide me throughout the rest of my life, to show me what was good and where there was evil. He came to know that, during His short time of parting His wisdom to me and took care to great length that "Dulkinna" remembers both at over-liminal and at subliminal level that force. That had become my guiding Light, my Shining Morning Star.....

23 years after his murder, "Dulkinna" wrote a poem about Him and the Big Thought Reading Machine and the game:

If I Could

I checked myself for the first time with a shrink, who begged me to not give in to the pain and mourning, to take the pills prescribed, but to just go and do whatever was pleasurable, whatever activity I still felt like participating in, while being an outpatient. We were running from the mountains to the seaside to visiting relatives in neighboring country of Moldavia. We were keeping busy with starting our own business, with dreaming big dreams of becoming industrious. Even love making was a way to hide the pain and then a way to be with the pain. Many times, after making love, I would burst in tears and Ioobe had to just hold me and strike my skin gently without saying much more than just: "I love you, you are my sweetness"

CHAPTER FOUR

The Big 'Voodoo'

After 24 years of marriage, we finally could finish each other's sentences as well. We almost never fought and Ioobe's attitude generally was: "tell me what would you like me to do to make you happy and I will do it". I never broke my secret vow. We called each other pet names and we were happy in almost every way. Almost.

In 1999 I was a financial analyst for a huge insurance company and things started seeming more and more weird to me, first at work and then in the family or when I was with friends. At first, I started noticing that I was just as big a starlet in the Southeastern American city of Atlanta, GA as I had been in my small city from Romania. And this time, it was not as warranted. It could not be because of my father being so popular and famous, or because my uncle had been a famous soccer player in his youth. This time I was an Ocean and a continent away from all that. So, I started thinking that as I was reading in some of my marketing journals and papers, I must be the subject of some secret marketing/management focus group, used to analyze the employee behavior. One, in which I was not told about my role, but where I was supervised 24/7 by my company's management, in order to learn about and improve the employee's performance….

Everybody in the company knew who Dulkinna was. She was better known than the CEO. People traveling to the headquarters from Latin

America or Europe, wanted to meet her and change a couple of words. She was a financial analyst, after all. What was all the attention and notoriety due to? When people asked her things about herself, she had the feeling in the beginning that I was meeting only kindred spirits, that we always understand each other. Gradually, I started thinking that they seem to be too knowledgeable about what I wanted for, what I would like to propose in a meeting, or after all, everything I was thinking of. It was gradually apparent that peers were proposing in meetings, the things I wanted to propose, so, I decided to stop making notes before a meeting and to only mentally make a couple of notes on the subjects I intended to talk about. They still seemed to "be in tune" with my thinking.....

About the same time, she started picking up signals from the TV. When dressing up in the morning, the morning show host used to comment on the very pieces of garment she was thinking about putting on. When going to work, she would notice that some people were dressed with the colors she was thinking about wearing, while others, with the colors that she finally chose to wear. THAT was a coincidence. Was the universe trying to give her a signal? Was she so in tune with the collective conscience that she was capable to influence their choice in garment colors? Had the company had installed cameras in her closets or elsewhere in the house, they could have know what she touched or moved around, but how do they manage to have a score of people dressed with the same colors she only thought of, but then changed her mind? Weird....

She and Ioobe never talked about having a child. She had had an abortion in college and never discussed the subject with her husband. It was taboo. Every time she tried to bring the subject of the children up, he would close her mouth by saying that "it is not yet the time". When friends and family wanted to know if they would like to have children, they would react differently. Ioobe always said: "maybe, latter" while Dulkinna used to say: "we don't know". At Mardi Grass time in 1999, they brought a cake to her office and all started talking about the baby being hidden in the cake. If you got the slice of cake with the baby in it, you would remain pregnant that year. It was before a "dragon" year by the Chinese zodiac and many people wanted to get pregnant. Useless to say, Dulkinna got the slice with the hidden baby doll.

That was too much. What do they want of her? This was beyond any marketing surveillance program of employees or focus groups. And how about her commenting for herself on their behavior and them picking up the subject and talking about it out loud? Was she subliminally linked to some of her co-workers? What type of hypnotic powers did she poses? How did she have such great intuition? She started thinking that they are employing voodoo priests to figure out what advertisements to through her way and what products she will use during the day. That same year, the movie "The Truman Show" came out. Nobody should have been aware of her paranoia yet. And though, they started questioning her about what she thought about the movie. They always talked to her in pairs. One person was always just witnessing any discussion she might have had with another.

That day, when she decided to make love to Ioobe, she started asking herself if somebody was watching. She was in the mood for something else, for more acrobatic moves and maybe in different rooms of the house. Maybe if she was not in the master bedroom they would not know what she was doing. She went to work after that. It was a Sunday and she wanted to start some programs to roll for the results to be ready for Monday morning. Eric was there and she just felt one of those thoughts. How did he know she had just had anal sex? What kind of people are these? Are there cameras in every room of the house? Not only in the master bedroom? Did the neighbors stake out the house? Were they in cahoots with the company?

They were no voices at that point, only thoughts that stood out like that, seemed out of place, but weren't. The kind that if you talked to somebody about, they would have labeled you as paranoid or crazy. What made her think that Eric knew about the anal sex? He knew. He even knew she knows. Where did she get such information? In his eyes. She heard his subliminal voice saying: "I am sorry to embarrass you like this, but today I must be the one reporting on you". She could not talk to Ioobe about this. She had mentioned the marketing tests she read about and he was very skeptical and asked her: "What, do you ever feel like somebody could actually watch us like that?" "Why would they do it' and "why would they not watch somebody more important, who are you for them to watch us like that?"

In 2000 it was so clear that they knew her thinking, that there were no secrets, of any kind, she attempted her first suicide. Everything had become routine. They were scolding her about what she was thinking, by pretending to have parallel conversations in which they would try to converse with her subliminal thinking. That year they traveled a lot. She was now on medication. The whole family had changed their attitude. In 89, when she went to the psychiatrist in Romania, they tried to convince her that that type of medication would affect her nervous system in negative ways and that she does not need it. Now, they all thought that medication was the most important thing in her life. By 2001, while vacationing in Romania, she started hearing their voices.

CHAPTER FIVE

What Do These People Want From Us?

After years, she started telling Ioobe about the voices in her head. He was always mentioning the need for medication. She had one way conversations now with the Dalai Lama, with the president of the America, with the queen of England and with Tom Cruise. Most often, she was mad at God, for allowing these people to keep her in the dark like that, at the Dalai Lama for condoning such deeds, while attempting to write about ethics for the new millennium, but most of all, she seemed to know about an owner of some sort.

She was now convinced that there was some sort of corporation, just like in the Truman Show, that knew and owned her. That could not have been a public company, she thought, that was a private holding. She ranted many, many nights at some hidden figure, telling him that one day, he will pay for the sacrilege. Well, the irony was wasted on that guy. Even she didn't know why. Nothing ever changed, anyway. Yet he was there, somewhere. Was he the owner of some huge mass media corporation? What was his problem? She felt protected and attacked by this man, at the same time. It was an unexplainable feeling. She rationalized that if she is his property, than he had every interest to keep her alive. But then, what was with the insistence on her taking medication ? By now, the side effects were so visible, she started shaking so much, that she was ashamed to go out in public. Yet, the doctor kept insisting that the dosages have to be increased.

When they moved to California, she changed doctors and decided to change her "game". She somehow understood that Ioobe will never be allowed to talk to her about the truth, but he knew enough in order to be aware that he needs to protect himself from these evil forces. So, when the doctors in the new places started asking about the voices, she invariably answered that there had been an episode, but that there are no voices any more. Besides, the voices started talking about killing her or even worse, about killing Ioobe.

At over-liminal level, the most weird thing was that they started making some new friends. Rumanian people, met at church fundraisers, at parties, at the grocery store, while speaking Rumanian. A couple of families, who pretended to be so charmed by Dulkinna, they could not have a social gathering without her present. She started having again the weird thoughts passing by: "What do you have in common with these imbeciles?", "They are a bunch of weirdoes, who want to take advantage of you and Ioobe". She always gently shushed the thoughts. They were hidden, somehow silent, not real voices. They were pretending to be her own creation, her deeper feelings, but she always knew better. That was no inner voice, those were passing voices that wanted to keep themselves hidden. To pretend they could at the right moment, make her take the wrong move, or decide on the spot to do something evil. They were just exercising their powers, trying to see how much influence can they have over her body, over her will, over her conscience.

In almost a sort of competition with the forces, Dulkinna was continually trying to explain just for herself the technology of the BIG THOUGHT READING MACHINE, as she could have understood it. Also, she vowed again, to maintain her mind healthy, her nervous system intact. The new doctor had to accept decreasing the dosage of the medication, since she constantly complained about the side effects of pills that were not needed since no new "psychotic episode" had been observed in years and years now. And the shaking stopped. She found a new job, but one that paid about a tenth of the hourly fees she was trained and ready to be earning. She figured, it was OK. Who would pay you for expressing at over-liminal level, only a fraction of the ideas that can be stolen from you subliminally? So, she figured the owner must have a plan. Maybe he figured she could not survive on tears alone and gave into the idea that she indeed might be happier just dressing up in the morning and having somewhere to go. The hiring manager had expressed the idea out loud.

An Electrical Engineer by training, with about four years of work experience in the telecommunications industry from Romania and then, having acquired her MBA in finance in America, she was constantly mixing and matching bits of new information, trying to figure what was the real game all about. How the machine might have worked and how the system could help people, but more importantly how it should be stopped from inadvertently hurting them. She had no idea that the system could actually turn all the way evil. She just kept pretending, that the potential for mistakes is so big, that society has become so vulnerable, that it is not worth staying "latent" any more.

In the mean time, she was pushing for obtaining a real job. It would have been the first sign that the machine HAS to ALLOW her to exercise her free will. This would have stood as a symbol of her fight for making sure, no other people can be used by the machine in the way she was. She wanted to check the ethical standards of the people in the system and the programmed functions of the machine. Are they going to try and show the intention of using the new technology for the good or for evil?

She was constantly thinking of the society becoming more and more dependent and driven by the machine, as in the Arnold Schwarzenegger movies. Gotham City and Batman, did not seem fictional any more. The danger was real, for these forces to actually bring "the eraser" to live, or to have an underground society that would have to fight for the right to eat a real egg and ham, as the traitor from "the Matrix" movie. Her boss had a sign in front of the entrance door, that read "welcome to paradise". Dulkinna in the late days with the company kept thinking that she will soon be connected with real bolts and hinges to the machine, just like Nemo and his girlfriend, fighting a Mr.. Anderson with a changing face, smiling always and always pretending to be your friend, only to try and suck on your brains. Finding the most creatively ingenious ideas, by questioning the subject at subliminal level, was now possible already. Dulkinna knew about this, because she "felt" the conversations going on in her subconscious at night.

She imagined the machine to be run by a system that was aware of the dangers. Yet, more and more, the system seemed to become overwhelmed by the evil forces. Her health started deteriorating. She was the asset, the lab rat. If she was dispensable, who will be forced to take her place? Was the machine getting ready to overtake "the stupids"? To make a subliminal slave of every engineer with creative ideas, every nerd without a business acumen, who was going to allow himself to believe that only Dulkinna could be "used", while "he" would always be a user? How much evil this could inflict in the society? Did she care? Why really? If people were calling her a cow, even while she was trying desperately to give them signs of "DANGER, do not come so close!" why did she even give a crap? It was for Him, for Ioobe and for the memory of those who went before her, rushing towards Heaven.

Somehow, the memory of her grandmother, uncles, cousin, father in law, mother in law, was powerful and shining as the stars in the sky, trying to remind her that she needed to maintain her integrity, that she should never be tempted. Yet, compared to the memory of her little brother, they were pale, if only flickers of internal light. He knew Ioobe and died knowing that Dulkinna will be with him till the end. This thought gave her the power to always fight for her marriage. The will to go on living, was for Ioobe's sake, when the fight against the machine seemed so useless, so evil skewed and so useless. Whenever she felt that going on was useless, she remembered: "what about Ioobe, how would he survive alone against the machine, what will the system do to him?, what about the feeling of abandonment, will he give in to those, if she was really successful in her suicide attempt?"

She was calling now to forces like the CIA, the FBI and the KGB or to Vladimir Putin. She was aware already that no call could ever go in vane. If she placed it, they came. It was "the spirit of the game". More and more, she became enamored by the Putin personality, by the fact that he seemed a strong hand for Russia and an intelligent leader, who knew how to manipulate the media, even while seeming to be a shy person. She started sending calls for help: "Could I, or may I be allowed to fight the machine?, she mostly started writing poems, about her never really bowing, her always keeping her head held high, her gaze reaching for the stars. Was this construed as insolence? Why the abandonment?"

Why was she reaching for such forces? Who knew? It was the internal voice. It was also the desperation, the flags and mental notes she secretly tried to make for herself, which signaled the war can be lost, if losing a couple of more battles. Her body was giving in. Her mental toughness gave place to a perpetual short on fuse frame of mind. She used to be able to drive them insane with her coolness. Now, she felt the point was moot. She was giving herself aneurysm after aneurysm trying to fight the system, trying to show to it the light, the right fight, the way to maintain the free spirit and the creativity alive.

All this time, she kept revisiting and revising her idea about the machine, the system and the game. She started writing guidelines for the new ethics in a world with the machine, for the system, for the society to follow, in the form of poems that she would email to herself, while imagining to having sent them to the forces that she kept trying to sway towards fighting THE battle, to winning THE war. People yawned and laughed. That meant: "yeah, yeah, we hear you cow.." She had to try harder, to awaken something in somebody important, to obtain a sign. Vladimir Putin sent it first. As she was showing some interest in Greek Mythology, the following day, she stumbled over a picture of Putin emerging from the ocean with a Greek amphora. The news of the day was that he went scuba diving and recovered some Greek artifacts. Could this have been? It was too big of a coincidence. Was he really giving a sign? Would he really manage to get himself reelected again, in his fight for offering Russia the liberties of free spirit and freedom of speech while keeping them from sliding back towards communism? What about that ugly longer than the building billionaire that wanted to oppose him? Would he have any success?

CHAPTER SIX

The Thanks Giving Trip to Las Vegas

Every year, it became tradition to take a trip to Las Vegas. Almost a must, to find out how the Bellagio interior garden had been decorated for the holidays. Then, a trip to the national parks. Dulkinna and Ioobe became in love with the beauty of the land of America. Back home, everybody speaks and knows the Grand Canyon, but they discovered so much more. The first love had been the Columbia River Gorge. That is where Dulkinna wanted first to know that some of her ashes could be scattered after she died. Ioobe took her to discover the Zion, Brice, Arches, Natural Bridges and Capitol Reef national parks. They had visited numerous times the "red and white stones" as Dulkinna called them. They loved the Yosemite, the Yellowstone, the Grand Tetons were a love at first sight. Hiking in the Sierra Nevadas was the most common thing they used to share.

In 2011, they took the usual trip. Dulkinna had wanted to spend the holidays at the vacation cottage in Arnold, but they decided it was better to get away, somewhere else. She wanted so much to go to the Indian reservations to see the slot canyons of the Lower Antelope and Upper Antelope Canyons again. Maybe take some "Peter Lick" pictures. She had discovered that son of a gun's art in the Venetian Casino in Las Vegas and they both fell in love with his way of capturing the light. With her cheap camera, always stubborn not to pay too much attention to the technical side of the endeavor, she wanted to take Peter Lick type picture, by following her instincts and her sense of beauty. The light would be proper in the Canyons some time in June, for that type of picture, but she never cares for this sort of limitation. A different beauty will be hers: same natural wonders, different light and picture taken with a cheaper camera.

The voices had become very interactive. She now had "conversations" with Vladimir Putin, the presidential candidate. He not only had heard the calls for help, but was telling her he wants to marry her. WHAT? She felt baffled and bemused, what was that about? Was he trying to compliment her? Why in such a way? It soon became apparent to her that some of the "uses" of the machine, was prevalent among the "know it alls" or the "aliens" as she used to call them. Apparently the machine could be used to create and give people a very powerful, unforgettable sexual experience. She had known about this for a while. It was almost the reason she did not enjoy making love any more. She knew they were always there. She stopped taking care of her body on purpose, to prevent the peep show. Yet, the practice seemed to be very much alive. Only they were doing it with the machine, even more than watching as she had initially feared.

She knew how to give herself an orgasm without even touching herself, without being together with Ioobe, just by contorting her body a little. The voices wanted to always witness that and she became scared. The first time, she woke up from her afternoon nap, to the voice of Tom Cruise guiding her through the act of giving herself an orgasm by using the machine which was working directly with her nervous system. The voice explained that he was just dipping his finger in a glass of water, to create the warm sexual sensation. The feeling was known to her already, but this was the first time the voice was offering an explanation of how the technology might have worked.

She had become so scared of them using the machine to "rape" her, that she almost gave up creating the opportunity for an orgasm when making love to Ioobe. She was asking him for sex and then just lay there, waiting for him to finish taking care of his business. She now could become ill with sexual desire. The opposite pole was reached. Now, she wanted sex and tried so hard to get her satisfaction before the act was over, only to try and evade that nausea, the feeling of so much sexual desire created artificially by the machine in her body, that she secreted almost fatal dosages of stress hormone.

It was nauseating to even hear the word sex. When thinking of it, she became instantly afraid. What if the desire becomes so horrendously real again?

Anyway, that might have been the motive for the new "love interest" from Vladimir Putin. She did not quite know what to make of it. The voices were now "coming clean", sort of speak, talking about a game that Dulkinna had been placed in, ever since before she had been born. Apparently, they were all these people that knew of her coming into the world. She was supposed to be a special child. That ringed true. She always liked her zodiacal signs. She was born in the year of the Snake and the month of the Leo. Whenever reading her zodiac, she always felt proudly comfortable with what was foretold. So, Vladimir Putin, telling her that he had been awaiting for her birth and actually had seen her travel through the birth canal, was only somewhat strange, wasn't it? The most weird stuff was yet to come.

Apparently, the really tall, ugly guy challenging Vladimir Putin for the Russian presidency in 2012 was someone who had know about Dulkinna for all of her life as well. He was calling himself the "husband to be". He was a playboy billionaire, who owned a huge holding company, with an entertainment wing also owning an American Basketball team. He was telling her this while she was riding along side Ioobe from Las Vegas to Sedona. He was making her feel warm inside and for some reason she did not really mind this time. What was that about? She was curios. He was telling her, that they had been born for each other and that his parents have told him that the mothers had met two years before the both of the children were born, in what was then, Leningrad, U.S.S.R. and had decided to have two children, a boy for Mikhail's mother and a girl for Dulkinna's mother, that were to be betrothed to each other. They never spoke after, but apparently, it just happened that two years later, the children were born, four months apart. A girl in Dulkinna's family and a boy in the Prokhorov family as the mothers promised each other.

Dulkinna was listening, smiling and wandering what will the voices "invent" next. He sounded so sweet though. On TV she had seen a rough, ugly, enormously tall guy, who was giving a speech in a very cold looking room, on the Russian Presidential Campaign trail. He asked her something, she did not remember what and all of a sudden she thought to herself: "I could have a son from you". She had started laughing at his middle name and had began imagining a little sweet boy, running around and her calling to him: "Dimitrovitch!". She dared fantasize, even if fully aware that the voices know her very feelings and her thinking the most new. She did not fully form a thought and the man asked her:

"Dulkinna, why do you feel that way?"

"What do you mean that way?"

"I am using the machine to block your thoughts, what were you feeling?"

"I knew that, I always knew you were aware of every thought and feeling I had"

"Yes, Dulkinna, it is called flabbergasting. I had been flabbergasting you since I was three years old. Remember your birthday cakes for your third birthday? I remember them too. I thought they were the best looking cakes I have ever seen. My big sister and I envied you for having those two cakes, like that"

"Fabber...sting..what?"

"Fla-bber-gas-ting Dulkinna, you will figure it out later, basically I can see and feel you from the distance. I know you are looking out the window now...what was that?..why do you say such things?"

Dulkinna had started wondering "why would the voices make fun of that Mikhail Prokhorov guy?"

"Dulkinna, it is me! I am that man! Please do not do such things, it is very hurtful. You have no idea for how long I have tried to be with you, woman."

He sounded sweet. She was thinking she should Google the guy.

"Yeah, do that! You know Dulkinna, there is more to it than what I just told you. It seems that My father and Ioobe were first cousins... what do you think of that?"

"What?"

"Remember the story your in laws had about the relatives in Leningrad who spoke about trying to be "coulturnaia", remember that family joke? That cousin of Ioobe was my father, Dulkinna."

"Yeah...OK"

"Dulkinna, I feel your sarcasm. Please do not do that! I cannot lie to you at subliminal level. It is the truth! Please believe what I tell you!.... Dulkinna, I have to tell you something. You will be my lawfully wedded wife...Dulkinna, how can you do that? How can you stop thinking like that?...what are you thinking of this? Dulkinna, are you OK?"

"Yep!"

"Dulkinna, you do not believe me. It is OK, you will see, do not worry about it now!..For now, I am just happy to be with you at subliminal level. But soon, I will come and take you by the hand and make you my lawfully wedded wife."

"Have I ever suggested that I am looking for a new husband?"

"Dulkinna, it is our destiny! I am in love with you and you will love me. You will see...Dulkinna, I know what you feel. Why do you say to yourself things like that?"

What was that about, she was thinking the machine has become too evil. She will never, never, never leave Ioobe. She would not want to live if he ever left her. She loved Ioobe. She loved Ioobe. Why in the world would she feel anything for this man? Who does he think he is with his money? These must be the flabbergastors, why would they make fun of that guy?

"Dulkinna, I am that man! Please believe what I tell you! We cannot lie to you at subliminal level. What I tell you is the truth."

"The culturnaia guy...so you are Ioobe's nephew from his first cousin?"

"Yes, Dulkinna, what do you think of that...My sister and I are your relatives from St. Petersburg that you always wanted to visit with. What do you think of the fact that I am a billionaire, Dulkinna?"

"A billionaire?"

"I own the Nets...have you heard of them?"

"Is that a baseball team?"

"Ha, ha, ha, basketball Dulkinna, basketball"

"Oh, I understand basketball better...never got to learn the rules of baseball"

"Ha, ha, ha..."

"You are so sweet...you sound so sweet"

"So, what do you think of that?...will you Google me? I will be with you tonight at subliminal level. Would you like that? Or would you rather be with Vladimir Putin?"

"She wants to be with Ioobe, she does not want to be with us... Dulkinna, why do you not want to believe what we are telling you?... Mikhail went of line, he cannot deal with you not wanting to belive him....Just Google him on your Ipad this evening when you get to the hotel."

CHAPTER SEVEN

Who Is This Billionaire?

At the hotel, Dulkinna could not wait to get in her bed and start Google-ing the guy. He had a PhD and owned a group called Onexim, but most links were related to the Nets basketball team, that he bought in 2008. She wanted to see the pictures. He was handsome. She liked his beautiful warm eyes and she loved his mouth. She did not know why. She almost could not breath. She knew he was on line and was hanging on her every thought and word that went through her mind... If this was indeed true..

"Dulkinna, I am that man!"

"God, All Mighty"

"Yes, I am here. You like me woman. You like my mouth you said? ...Dulkinna, how do you do that? There is nothing, you are not saying anything at subliminal level? Are you?.. Woman, you said yes at subliminal level."

"You said you cannot lie.."

"I know, I am over-liminal, I am speaking out loud to the machine, Dulkinna. If I do that, I can jokingly lie to you. Do you know that you answered yes to my question?"

"Yes, I felt that!"

"God All Mighty Dulkinna!"

"You love my eyes woman, why?"

"I don't know, they are warm..she thought...weird"

"Weird, that I know what you are thinking? Those are your subliminal answers Dulkinna, you cannot lie to the machine or the flabbergastor. We always know everything you feel, everything you are thinking of, even before you know, or finalize the thought. We take that information from your spinal cord."

"I know"

"How do you know?"

"I know!" she shrugged her shoulders.

"She knows!" the voices said.

"who else is on line?"

"your flabbergastors and the people of the system, Dulkinna; I am your flabbergastor universal and your husband to be...you like me very much Dulkinna."

How strange it was, to look at a man's picture and for him to feel everything you feel or think about him, like that-she thought before falling asleep. The voices went quiet.

The next morning, she went swimming in the hotel swimming pool. He was with her, she knew it. In the beginning he did not say anything. Then, he started to woo her with that sweet voice of his. She was amazed. He looked more rough, but the voice was that of an adolescent almost....

"This is my voice at subliminal level, from when I first fell in love with you Dulkinna!..Would you like to know when that was?"

"When?"

"Do you remember that day when Ioobe gave you oral sex for the first time?"

"Excuse me?" she blushed, she had to go to the margin of the pool to hang on to something.

"you blushed woman. I remember that day, you were in love with Ioobe. I was there too...you looked so good, the way you lay on that bed and thinking that Ioobe must really love you to be such a giving lover...I fell in love with you then!"

She started looking at the people around the pool. They were on line. Some were smiling. She could see some smirks. They knew she felt uncomfortable. She could see how some were trying to avoid her gaze, to give her the illusion of privacy, while others were more curios, they wanted to look directly into her eyes to check on the accuracy of the machine. Those were the worst to bear. The nonbelievers, the ones that had the link to the secret machine and still wanted to check on what was going on. They had no idea how much they were hurting her nervous system. Not everybody understood how the machine was working directly with her nervous system. People were mostly treating her as if she were an avatar. As if this were a video game. Others thought of her as the star of a different kind of reality show. She never had access to the show. She would not have known how to get to her web-page on the internet. But she knew it was there. As in the Truman Show movie, she sometimes was thinking:

"Now they should all start paddling on their bicycles, waving to the cameras that were filming from the satellite".

How she wanted to see that day when she could say: "Good afternoon, good evening and good night". Sometimes she felt so alone. She could never talk with anyone about the machine, about the voices about the system at over-liminal level.

She kept telling them that the system ought to be over-liminal. How were the people dealing with this big lie? She knew, they were so entrenched in the thinking that all these awful things were done unto her, they did not take into consideration their own vulnerability in front of the machine. People were having fun, listening to Mikhail and Dulkinna at subliminal level, they did not fathom the degree of lack of privacy in their own lives. They kept pretending.

And the ones who realized the vastness of the issue, were so outraged, they wanted her dead. They figured, without her, the machine would not function properly. They had to get rid of that evil machine. Simplest way: to kill her dead.

Others wanted her dead for a different issue. They felt sorry for her. They felt her pain and wanted her to stop suffering.

She loved them all. Not the same, but she could understand the different points of view. Sometime in the past she used to beg Vladimir Putin, that if she would be killed, they shoot her execution stile. She used to ask for her own KGB agent, to mercifully kill her. She had made her will, sort of speak, by asking that nobody cry for her the way she had cried for her departed brother. She begged and asked Ioobe numerous times at over-liminal level, that if she ever died an untimely death, he remarries and never cries for her. So, she can at least get to Heaven and rest in peace in the other world.

CHAPTER EIGHT

Am I In Love With You? Who Is In love With Whom? Who Had Whom At Hello?

Every morning when she woke up she was asking:

"Mikhail, are you there?"

"Good morning Dulkinna!"

"what time is it?"

"what? I was not paying attention, I am doing something now."

"Are you working?"

"No, woman, I wanted you!"

"Mikhail, are you making love?"

"Not now, Dulkinna!"

"OK, have fun"

"What is that supposed to mean woman?"

"Nothing, I thought you were with a lady"

"and I was, but now I am with you. What was that supposed to mean? Are you not jealous?

"why should I be jealous?"

"Dulkinna, this is not just a fantasy. You will be my lawfully wedded wife. I love you, you will see when I come to pick you by the hand.. Please pretend that you will divorce Ioobe"

"Do you realize how much you do ask of me?"

"I do, woman, but this is our destiny. We were made for each other Dulkinna. When you make love to Ioobe I feel like I want to kill something. Why can't you be jealous at all when I am with another woman?"

"I do not know, I just am not, but please do not ask me to divorce Ioobe. I love him and I cannot live without him."

"Dulkinna, do you want to become over-liminal?"

"Yes, I do, but what does that have to do with our divorcing each other? If you loved me, you would want me to fulfill my mission. You know I have to help bring the system over-liminal. To announce the existence of the Big Thought Reading Machine. Do you know how much I want that ?"

"Why, why do you care about that?"

"Because...I want ...aaa... better place... this world to be. Do you understand how important this is for the future generation, for this generation? The machine and the technology are too advanced. If no limitations are put on the system at over-liminal level, if Congress does not start making laws for dealing with the new power people have of influencing each other's life at subliminal level, the world could end in a couple of years maybe. Can you imagine what would happen if I died and did not try to bring the system over-liminal? Do you realize the fighting, the lieing the finger pointing? It would take years to create some laws and then, who would administer the system? The first lady? The secretary of state? This would mean a militarized America. If I fight for taking the system over-liminal, I can ensure that there is a smooth transition, you can help me!"

"I love you when you get like that, woman. You will be my lawfully wedded wife, you'll see"

"Really"

"Yeah, bitch, I had you at hello!"

"You had me at hello? Or I had you at hello? How does that work?"

"Either way bitch, I told you: we were made for each other"

"So, who had whom at hello?"

"Ha, ha, ha..you are a lot of fun woman, I cannot believe my luck!"

"Mikhail, you told me we have children."

"Yes, remember when you went to check to see if you were ovulating, if you could have children?"

"Yes"

"That is when they harvested your eggs. Together with the Dimitrovitch that you want, we would have 250 children"

"How is that possible?"

"I don't know, ask the KGB and Vladimir Putin and Michelle Clinton. I never knew about them until now either!"

"Is it true?"

"Yes, Dulkinna, it is true!"

"God All Mighty, I cannot wait to meet them!"

"I know woman, we all know that"

"Why am I not over-liminal yet?"

"Because I do not know how to bring that about. Vladimir Putin does not want to guarantee to me that you will be safe at over-liminal level. We would have to live in Moscow. That is where my business holdings are."

"What about St. Petersburg?"

"St Petersburg? Why St. Petersburg?"

"I always wanted to see Aurora Borealis in St. Petersburg"

She started writing a poem on her Ipad.

I Wished For A Trip To St. Petersburg
I planed long time ago,
My trip to see Aurora Borealis.
I wanted that foreign country to see,
With the alphabet so strange and people like me.

I would like to have seen Hermitage,
Nevsky they say is touristy.
This year I went to Paris instead,
There, I definitely know "the alphabet".

My fear I should conquer, I hope
To someday see the Mir bookshop,
Maybe this poem to see,
In a book published by me.

Babushkas and children alike I would watch,
I would reckon the 'protipendade',
Would I buy postcards or not,
I know I would love it a lot.

Yet, what about that alphabet?
I cannot decipher it yet!
Who would buy me the bread?
Would they give me cake instead?

Palace square I would take pictures of,
I do this, when I wander about,
To see the world, to know the people,
To learn how to say: 'I am glad'.

'Pajalusta' they would respond,
Eating galupti and borsh,
I would then say: 'so long'
They would reply: 'would you stay?'

"We have to gather the children, woman, they are scattered all over the world. People are hurting them. They wanted to have your egg, to have your children and now they are hurting them, trying to ask for money for them. How are we going to raise 250 children woman?"

"We will build a compound. A high rise and will pretend to be living there with our children and their surrogate families"

"We'll pretend woman, we'll pretend."

"Will we do this?"

"Dulkinna, the children are real!"

"I understand that all these women wanted your children, to marry you, but why mine?"

"People like you, Dulkinna. They say you are the salt of the earth. Good as goodness is, woman. You are good as warm bread, as they say in Romania, remember?"

"Yes, I know that expression: 'buna ca painea calda'".
"This is who you are woman, the 'darling of America'"

She thought, of the 2000 trip to Hollywood boulevard and when Ioobe's cousin had pretended to call her that, while sitting on the star of Doris Day. Where did the time flie? It was like yesterday, that she was on hunger strike, demanding at subliminal level that they end the Voodoo. 12 more years have passed and the system is still not over-liminal. She would have white hair is she did not dye it now. And, she has to start a new life, to raise 250 children together with Ioobe and Mikhail. What a task! She has to bring the system over-liminal. If only the Games would end. If only people would start thinking about the serious stuff. If they would not allow themselves brainwashed like they are now, by the prospect of winning these lotteries...
"God, All Mighty!"

CHAPTER NINE

What, How, Where Went Wrong?

On Friday, March 30th, 2012 Dulkinna had a great day. She went skiing with Ioobe and while she was waiting for him to finish his final rounds, she was writing poetry on her Ipad at the lodge and playing the game with the system in her head. The game was coming together so well, that she was almost exalted. She was always reluctant to play, but then she usually got into it. And then, even the voices could not stop her. That day, Mikhail who was the owner and father of the game, wanted to finally have a great game, with the big winner. As the game progressed, Dulkinna kept being more and more in awe at what a great game she was putting together and how amazingly easy and elegant everything was flowing together. The winner of the game emerged to be Dulkinna's Goddaughter, Filipa. She had won the biggest prize ever awarded in the game. Mikhail was promising Dulkinna that they would come that day and bring her over-liminal.

They went back to the vacation home in the village and Dulkinna started to prance around, thinking she should continue with something just as pleasant. She loved to cook. Her vacation home was filled with all the utensils and pots and pans that she loved. Any time she bought something new, she took it to the vacation home. She liked to feel as if it were a holiday, every time they went up in the mountains.

She started cooking two or three entrees and a cake. While cooking, the voices always kept her company. That was always a big game. Always, nobody wanted to miss a move that she made while cooking. She had to pay attention to the cooking and to the game. The voices were not allowed to help themselves while she cooked, but after she did something that hurt someone's game, the voices usually made a big fuss. Usually they just tried, in principle, to make her trip. They loved to criticize her. Not that day.

The voices seemed very happy and agreeable and kept talking about the President himself coming to take her over-liminal, after declaring the end of the game in America. Mikhail promised he would be there to take her by the hand. She was baking, cooking, mixing the cream for the cake, prancing around happy, happy, happy.

Then, the voice of the flabbergastess said that she would like to propose that the game of the day be void, since a family member should not have won the big prize. Dulkinna became focused on the voices.

"what is going on?"

"I do not think a family member should have won the big prize"

"Do you understand that the game was impeccable and it followed the spirit of the game? Do you realize that this is now cheating in the game?"

"I want to have my own game, to have the opportunity to win the big prize, it is unfair to give it to a family member"

"Do you understand that this is my personal money that I would get for becoming over-liminal, that my husband to be wanted to offer a big prize from?"

"???. . . . ."

"She actually thinks she is becoming over-liminal" the voices said finally.

She was becoming desperate, tried to maintain her cool. She could identify the usual symptoms and became afraid. Tried to focus again on the cream for the cake.

The machine started swirling again. The system did not make any sense for a short while. Then the flabbergastess again and the voice of the first lady who announced that she agrees that the prize should not be awarded to a family member.

This was too evil. Too EVIL she shrugged, went to the medicine cabinet, opened the medicine bottle and a glass of red wine. She did not have enough medicine at the vacation home. She figured:

"I need another glass of red wine, that will speed up the poisoning process"

She figured she would clean up after she wakes up if she does not die this time either and rushed to bed. She was dizzy within seconds. She went to the bedroom, put on her pajama bottoms and placed the top next to her.

"I do not have the power to put this on.." her head fell heavy on the pillow.

....

... "She will need her boots, she might be cold"

....

... "They must be taking me to the hospital, I am probably on the girdle"

....

"I will now pretend to be Mikhail Prokhorov.."
"No"
"what do you mean no?"

....

... "I will now wash her hair"

....

... "We will take your picture now for the file"

....

.... "Could you stand up for me and choose a bed?"

....

"Good morning, today is Monday, April 2nd, you are in the hospital, you have tried to commit suicide. Do you remember anything?"

I Am Alive Again

I breathe, so I must be,
I think, I know for sure,
But it is not the same,
As it was before.

In some ways I am glad,
In others I am scared,
But I wish I remembered
What have I done to myself.

I remember the rage,
The pills and red wine,
But I do not understand
The numbness of my mind.

People say they care,
I pretend to listen,
Yet I a do not really care,
For their parting wisdom.

Disappointments and disgrace,
Lack of satisfaction,
I did not evade,
Only lack of action.

I will not try again,
Yet not happy, still,
I decided from now,
I will not prophecies fulfill!

Better let them try,
Let them be the ones,
To give the bad news,
To pretend to care.

What Do I Feel

What do I feel?
What substance is this?
Is it true?
Is there only bliss or abyss?

Am I the last to always know it?
I wish sometimes,
more clearly you would show it!

Forgive the indiscretion,
But was it your wish?
I cannot believe,
You want me to conceive.

Such notion is strange,
To me and to others,
I want your wish, your guidance,
Your love.

I do not know how,
But I still am trying,
Your word to listen,
Your message to hasten.

I think, than change my mind,
I sip and swallow,
I walk then to follow,
Is numbness required?
Or is it just for now,
To bring about patience,
To learn about Prudence?

I will follow through,
I will see it all that I can,

Please do not punish,
Please! No skirmish!

Let it be more light,
Let it be more easy,
Let it show more clear
For each of them to see!

"THIS GROUP SESSION IS OVER, YOU MAY GO TO YOUR
BED NOW!"

CHAPTER TEN

I Remember Aborting My Child

When I became pregnant it was not by mistake. I actually wanted a child. I was head over hills in love with the man I was dating. His name was Nelu and he was my high school sweetheart. He was extremely handsome, very tall, with dark big eyes and a well build body. I don't remember much about him any more, except that at the time I was crazy about him. He was a high school dropout and played professional volleyball.

When we became sexually involved, I was almost 18 years old and he had just enrolled in the army. I was solving 200 mathematics and physics problems a week and writing love letters.

When I started college at the School of Electrical Engineering of the Polytechnic Institute of Bucharest, I began having issues with my boyfriend not having graduating high-school. I was afraid I would have to leave him and probably in the purest of my personal styles, I instinctively felt that I need to sabotage my place in society.

The night that I became pregnant, was the night of the Rookie ball at my college. All my friends told me that day that if I go, they intend to vote for me to become queen of the ball. Instead, I decided to stay in my dorm and make love to my boyfriend of whom, only trusted friends knew about. He was on permission from the army and he came to visit me and take me to the ball. For all the time we dated, we kept it a secret because of my parents. In fact, my parents knew of him but always referred to him as the fatherless boy. This is what my father called him. I was so disappointed with my parents, that I don't think I ever told them that Nelu did not graduate from high school. They probably just knew that he was not in college yet.

That night we kept asking ourselves weather to go to the ball and tell all my friends about our relationship. I had a brand new tailored dress just for the occasion. Instead, we ended up making love all evening and all night and I was asking for a baby the whole time. I still remember his face in awe while listening to me. For a couple of hours, we really believed we would ignore all the rules of the Romanian society and live happily ever after.

When I found out that I was indeed pregnant, reality immediately kicked in. In the eastern, Romanian society, that child would have been a flower child and I would have been an outcast, a woman without morals. I went to a school where women were in minority. The school was generally considered a manly one. I decided to use my college years to have fun instead of affirming myself…

I had proven myself in the Math and Physics High-school that I had graduated in my hometown. My classmates used to be outraged at my telling the professors to stop with proving certain problems because the solution had become self evident already. My classmates informed me that not everybody was as clever as I was and they would like the professor to talk to the end.

One time, in math class, the professor was focusing on something else and I was having a conversation with my friend Alina. He raised his glance and noticed me. He called on me to go to the blackboard and gave me a difficult problem to solve. Then, he started thinking of how the problem should be solved. By the time he started talking about it, while turning his head toward me, the solution was already circled on the blackboard. He became outraged, he started raving at me that by the time I graduated I would not know how to cook and make pickles. He expelled me from his class, until I had my father come talk to him. He was also the adjunct manager of the High School. Instead of telling my father, I used to stay in the library and solve physics problems during my math hour. The librarian, decided to talk to my father herself after a week. She wanted to save both my teacher's ego and mine.

So… I had been a geek in high school and I did not want to be one any more. Everything seemed to make sense in the way that my father had projected. He taught me that in college will be a time to shape myself from a societal point of view. He once came to my dorm one Saturday evening and found my friend and cousin Simmone and I revisiting our notes. He was disappointed. He told us that was a job to do during the rest of the week and during weekends, we should go see a movie or a theater play if we did not have a party to tend to. During those years I admired him very much. I was willing to close my eyes at his faults and was happy to have a very open minded father. From that Saturday on, Simmone and I never spent a weekend without going to a party for the rest of the year.

Simmone never knew that I had been pregnant, never knew of my abortion. Not from myself, anyway. The thing that I reproach most to Nelu was that he did not help me enough with my abortion. He kept lying to me about procuring some pills, then some injections and the time had passed and I had to go for intrusive abortion when I was three months and a half pregnant. In my heart, I wanted that child even the night before the procedure. Abortion was illegal in Romania at that time, mine was done in an apartment studio by two women whose names I did not know. It was arranged by a friend of my best friend Violeta.

My abortion played a very important role in my life. I love children dearly. I am now 47 years old and I smile whenever I see a woman pregnant or a young mother handling her baby or toddler. I wanted my baby and yet I went for an illegal abortion that left me barren.

Today, I think that abortion should be absolutely legal and yet I do not advise any woman to ever go for one. It is the most awful thing a woman could ever feel, to suffer such physical pain in order to kill her own baby. It makes no logical sense and I think having had the "choice" from a legal stand point, I would have opted otherwise. I had nobody to talk to who could help me raise my baby.

The night of the abortion, I was closer to death than I could have ever imagined. The doctors who performed my hysterectomy after my hemorrhage almost killed me, were all trying to save me as if I were part of their own family. They did not have enough blood for the transfusion so they mixed plasma in order to save me. They wept for me and I was weeping for my baby and my parents. Violeta had been the one who decided to take me to the hospital after seeing how blood was running out of me. She risked her freedom, while saving my life. The doctors could have called the authorities and we could have both been imprisoned for the abortion. Instead, all those doctors fraternized with us and decided to work all night to help stabilize me and keep me alive. In the morning they told me that the official diagnosis would be an infection of the uterus. They trew it away, in case authorities would come to perform a test on it, on account of having smelled too badly. As I write about this, I remember my hemorrhage, how blood was coming out of me, as I was filling a bucket. I also remember the doctors fearing for my life and my telling them that my father had hart problems, so they should not be too blunt when giving the bad news. But the most terrible thing I remember, was the two women performing the abortion, describing it to each other and talking about a little hand of the fetus. When I became interested they shut up and were amazed that I still wanted that child even as it was being butchered inside me. My child would have been older now than I was when having the abortion. They never told me whether it was a boy or a girl. So, like in Plato's Republic, I look at every 29 year old and think I could have had a sun or a daughter. Maybe I would have been a grandmother already. What kind of mother would I have been? I'll never know, but **I will never stop wanting to hold my baby in my arms.**

CHAPTER ELEVEN

What Is Good And What Is Evil?

Is goodness to be thought of as from the bottom of my heart, or is it the rational deed, inspired by my wise mind? If I use my cortex and not only my instinctual feelings, am I guilty of evil manipulation? What I want, can it be evil? If I want it right now, only the way I feel about it, can it really be called evil? Say, I want to look prettier than my friend, for the Christmas party, is that little bit of vanity, used to satisfy my ego and sooth my soul, an evil thought? Hardly! Yet, if all I ever thought about, all I ever counted as important, all I ever valued, my comparison with my friend in beauty, the Bible says, I would be evil and cursed. I happen to agree.

First, what friendship would that be? If my friend asked my opinion for what dress to wear, I would have to take into account that God forbid, she should never look better than I. And that, right there, would poison my thought. To do that even once, for the Christmas party, would still be evil. The way to sooth my ego would be," If she looks that good, I'd have to look my best too." That to me sounds acceptable. I do not really have to always advertise my best friends looks, even while" loving my neighbor" as the Bible says. Yet, telling her that the color yellow, which makes her complexion look too pale, is the best one to choose for the party, is evil. The thinking that it is just a Christmas party, no big deal, she should not be so vane, is even more evil. Rationalizing other people's deeds, while always defending all of ours, goes right out to breaking the Ten Commandments. If you try to think about it, you always break one of them in such an instance. Most of the time is the one where you wish for your neighbor's wife, or house or goat. The Bible says that is evil and that if doing that, one is cursed and Deuteronomy even gives us the punishments for such deeds.

Is it easy to fall into the trap, to fall into temptation? Oh, yeah!

What about my heart desires? Do I have to ignore my instincts? No! But there are limits and ethical standards to follow and believe it or not, I found that the easiest ones to follow, for me, are coming from the Bible. As harsh as it sounds, not breaking The Commandments or not committing the Deadly Sins, seems to be somewhat ingrained in every one of our DNA's. All we usually have to do, is take a deep breath and take stock. Is compassion stupid thinking? Putting yourself in the other one's shoes is that out of date and downright imbecile in today's dog eat dog world? No matter how much one wants for something, one always seems to know if evil or the Devil has managed to make us tempted. Expressions like "a little evil thought" or "you little devil", used jokingly and lovingly in every day life, are OK, as long as you do not start thinking that "a little evilness is necessary".

In today's society, for a 50-year-old man to marry a sixteen old girl is considered wrong. Is it evil? It depends. It certainly does sound controversial enough to raise a lot of eyebrows. However, I really know women, who absolutely look for a father figure in their spouse and are never happy with someone their own age. Just food for thought! Now, how about the same sixteen year old looking to take my 50-year-old husband? Weee..ell? How about the 50 year old husband who decides to make a move on the sixteen year old? This one is easier to judge is it not? For me anyway, it is.

Let us return though to the sixteen-year-old beauty, who loves a father figure. After all, this is what she really wants, let us assume, that we have hindsight and that she really is the type that would not be happy with a 20-year-old young man. Should she know better? Yes, she should. It does not matter that her heart desires. My heart desires cake and that is OK. But gluttony is what is evil. Not that one desires a piece of cake or a cup of ambrosia. The desire for the cup of ambrosia is what makes us human, what teaches us the beauty of life. Deciding that ambrosia should only be for ourselves and never allowed to others, that is what pushes us into abyss.

Societies around the world define right and wrong behavior in more strict or lax ways, we call them less or more civilized. A grandmother never showed her hair in public. Is a five year old, hiding his grandmother's burqa evil? She would certainly consider he was a little devil and probably never leave the house during that day. How about a twenty year old, who never wants to follow her parents advice and go out without covering her hair? Society has advanced, other girls in class do not cover themselves, is it evil, is it just parting from tradition? Should she have a choice? Should society make that choice available to her? At what cost? How much is lost and how much is gained, does it matter? These are not easy to answer questions. But there is always a distinction between wrong and outright evil. And we always, always, have it ingrained in our DNA, sort of speak. We know when we hurt others with our wants and choices. We absolutely know the difference between real hurt and simple inconvenience if we really listen to our wise mind. We can recognize that evil thought from early childhood even.

When being "good" becomes "silly" at worst, when society (peers) start considering it "stupid" as a matter of fact, that is when evil really starts creeping into our minds and souls. Today we have to be tough! Strong! For example, as managers, we have to fire people. Declaring "I will never do that", in today America, is almost weak. But, now, let us say, you have an employee who is the only bread earner, with five children, a handicapped or terminally ill wife and has been a little down lately. Maybe not even performed up to his personal best. I fire him tomorrow? Tell him that life is not fair, or that it is tough? Now, THAT is evil! There, I draw the line. After all, corporations have to function in society, just like people. So, if they are people too, I can accommodate and give a little slack to my fellow man. Is resigning yourself, knowing that you have a better chance of getting maybe even better pay and finding another job faster stupid? Not really. The corporate office might even keep the both of you and offer the good manager, you, a promotion. We ARE human and we HAVE to function in society and ARE NOT ALLOWED to forget that.

Should I expect same kind of morals from my fellow men? Yes, but I should not really hold my breath for it. Life is unfair, but we absolutely have to make our own choices, choose our own battles, make or not make our own compromises. A little white lie might be OK, but: "Honey you *absolutely have to wear the yellow dress, it makes your eyes sparkle"* CAN *be evil! Depending on the situation, I always choose for myself.*

Dulkinna stopped writing in her autobiographical novel, it was late, time to eat and go to sleep....

CHAPTER TWELVE

The Anchor

Through her subliminal conversations with her husband to be, Mikhail Dimitrievitch Prokhorov, Dulkinna has found out that she was the anchor for the Big Thought Reading Machine.

"Does this mean what I think it means?"

"Yes, Dulkinna, the machine works with your DNA. You are practically the central nervous system of the machine"

"This is why I am so sensitive lately to every word, everybody says on the system"

"Exactly!"

She was curious how Mikhail has worked towards fulfilling his destiny, as he puts it every time they talk. She had heard from Michelle Clinton, that Mikhail had built her a "home" near San Petersburg, in his native Rusia.

"A palace complete with hundreds of bedrooms for our children that had been conceived in vitro at Hillary Obama's orders and raised by the surrogate parents."

One of those that Mikhail managed to invite to live with him in the palace, was Nadina Taga. She was the natural daughter of Dulkinna with Ioobe. She had a very high IQ, just like her parents and was in love with her natural father's passion for computing and especially for the Big Thought Reading Machine. At 21, Nadina showed wonderful potential for becoming the next anchor. To Nadina the machine was not previously denied. She could defend herself from the ineptitudes of various programmers or the sheer hate and envy of the fame seekers.

"How is Nadina?"

"I am fine mother, I am awake, you can talk to me directly"

"Hi sweetheart, have you thought about the project your dad proposed to you?"

"Yes, I decided to make myself the next anchor for the Big Thought Reading Machine, but only after you and dad become over-liminal".

"You are a clever child!"

"I want to see that the world respects the rights of the anchor, I want to see them respecting your health, your nervous system and then, I will put myself out there for them."

Dulkinna had been 'attacked' numerous times, at subliminal level. She had been 'fattened' by a jealous first lady, Hillary Obama and her system had numerous times been under attack from various hackers. Both Dulkinna and Ioobe have requested the system to stop these attacks, warning that the anchor demise, means no system for the people to use, but their cries went in vain. Nadina new by now, what her mother had to put up with. Dulkinna had been fattened almost 100 lbs artificially and had been given various diseases by the fickle and the hateful.

"I decided to listen to you and father, but first you should hear Mikhail's surprise for you, mother!"

"We have your network Dulkinna. I have organized the network the way you wanted, based on the perfection of the honeycomb."

"Everybody now knows the truth mother!" Dulkinna had tears in her eyes. She could feel the joy and excitement in her daughter. For a second they had been in complete and direct communication at subliminal level.

"Oh, mother, I can feel your warmth, you are pleased!"

"Oh God, woman, Oh God, yes, I was with you too, Nadina gave you to me, God it is good to feel your warmth! You have no idea how you make other people feel!"

"Why are you doing that?"

"We are the Navy! We have to protect the anchor! The hackers are on to you, they could come to attack her through you! You cannot be in direct connection with her at subliminal level any more."

"Through the mesh around me, please use my mesh!" Dulkinna shrieked, afraid of the hackers.

"Do not worry madam, this is why you hear us so faintly, we are using the mesh and we are hovering you!"

Dulkinna had asked Mikhail to build a strong network and to take notes for a new machine without an anchor, a third generation machine. After building an anchor for herself, Nadina and her brother Alex, would start working on the final version of the machine, that would not use anybody as an anchor any more. But this dream was yet far from being reached. Dulkinna was worried about her demise at the hands of the hackers or a hater and leaving her children without defense, in a world full with Goulds. The machine was the only defense against those initiated in the practice of hurting others in order to supposedly become stronger at subliminal level, to better themselves.

"We have to show the world that by hurting others, you can only become weaker and weaker, at subliminal level"

"People are fickle Dulkinna"

'They are going to come along if you have indeed built the network and as they see that you can be stronger and stronger when you put your trust in God"

"Madam, please do not talk about God, people do not believe in God like you do!"

"Really? And what other way is out there to believe in God?"

"Has your God helped you when Hillary Obama decided to fatten you?"

"God works in mysterious ways" muttered Dulkinna to herself.

"If you think so"

"We were Queens of Sheba on Madonna's network and we never gained weight. We managed to better ourselves. You have to kill in order to be able to better yourself. This is nonsense what you tell us with your belief in God!"

"Really, how healthy is Madonna? I know she is skinny, but is she in perfect health?"

"No, she is not, is she?" shouted Mikhail.

"Just remember: you cannot break rank! No matter what happens, do not break rank, maintain the integrity of the network and you will always be able to defend yourselves against the Goulds."

"Is she not a Goauld? How come she is not dead, with all the attacks?"

"The anchor has never killed, she repairs herself, is of superior intelligence, knows instinctively how to repair herself, but if attacked incessantly at subliminal level, she will succumb. Do not attack my anchor, or you will feel the curse of the navy, on the system!"

CHAPTER THIRTEEN

Is This My Child?

One of the technological advancements in the age of the Machine was in the medical field. Going to gynecology has become a nightmare for any expecting mother. Women have found themselves giving birth to babies that had unfamiliar traits and features and they had no idea that they had been artificially inseminated.

During games and shows, Dulkinna has uncovered that some of her friends had no idea if the children they had given birth to, were produced through natural or artificial insemination. And they did not seem to care.

"They can change the fetus inside you, with a different one, obtained from a petrie dish"

"What do you mean?"

"Just do not fall asleep while at the gynecologist and you will be fine"

"This is not true!"

"Really? Than what does the system say that it is all true?"

"Do you understand that Carmina did not know that she had been inseminated with Dulkinna's baby?"

"I know when they did this! I fell asleep in the doctor's office, that is when they had changed my baby with hers."

"You are raising your own baby, you imbecile and you do not even know it"

"Do you understand that my baby was in love with Dulkinna, the first time I allowed her to hold it?"

"So what?"

"The baby had just felt her warmth, you morons"

"Mr. Kauffman, is this true?"

"It is true!"

"How could you not know if you were artificially inseminated?"

"I did not go to the gynecologist until I was three months pregnant, they changed the fetus, not the embryo?"

"Are you kidding us?"

"You still do not want the Tsarina over-liminal?"

"No, Mr. Putin! This is preposterous. The child of Carmina looks like his father, everybody can see that on the system."

"The child looks like Dulkinna's grandfather. The one who promised Adina that he will be reborn before his daughter goes to Heaven."

"The one who allowed himself killed by the haters so that Linu would be allowed to live?"

"Precisely" came the voice of the system.

"But why?"

"Carmina wanted the baby of Ioobe, yet Michelle had denied her in the beginning. This way, the women never know whose baby they have given birth to, yet, when they investigate, they cannot sue, because they requested for the procedure at some point."

"Are you trying to tell me, that Dulkinna grandfather's soul had found a way to be reborn while she was still in this world and in one of the families close to her?"

"He came to be close to her"

"Really? What about her religion? This does not hold water in Christianity and she keeps touting her Christian Orthodoxy, does she not?"

"Do you hear her talking?"

"It is true, Dulkinna, how do you explain that?"

"God works in mysterious ways", she said puzzled.

CHAPTER FOURTEEN

Remembering The Summer Of 2012 (The Cannibalism)

It was during or right before the Olympics. Dulkinna was constantly being promised by the handsome husband to be, that she will become over-liminal. She was somewhat circumspect. Maybe because they were from time to time in direct communication at subliminal level, she could feel that he is trying to keep her spirits up.

"How would you like to become over-liminal and accompany me to the Olympics, Dulkinna?"

"That would mean I could be with you and invoke Dimitrovitch?"

"Ay, ay, ay Dulkinna! What about myself? I do not exist for you without those kids?"

"Why would you ask me that? Do you not know everything I feel?"

"I do, you love me woman? That is what you said at subliminal level. I love you too."

"I know, I felt it!"

"That is called your under-liminal level, Dulkinna. At subliminal level you directly told me that you love me!"

"I think I know that too. Sometimes it is like I hear a deeper voice while I talk to you, but sometimes I do not. It is very strange, how you get this information out of me at subliminal level and I am not always aware of it. This time, I tell you that I was!"

"If you say so…How do you know that?"

"He does not believe me"

"Who said that, I am Dulkinna, who said that?"

"You did, madam, at under-liminal level"

"No, I do not think so, that was flabbergastation."

"It was you, madam, they just brought your under-liminal at over-liminal level faster than you would have"

"Please stop doing that, it is very annoying. You are hurting me! It feels familiar and yet, it seems strange. About the Olympics…"

"Yes, Dulkinna?"

"Please stop asking me. You know there is no time to bring me over-liminal. You have to pay attention. I am so afraid of it. Something terrible will happen and I cannot put my finger on it. Please pay attention to what is happening around you!"

"Are you afraid of terrorism, you mean"

"No, I do not think it is terrorism, but I am afraid of something terrible"

And then, during the show of the opening ceremony, there it was. Dulkinna could not believe it, THE CHILDREN! God All Mighty, something terrible is being done to my children. She could not explain that silly display of children on beds and the baby in the center…what was that about? She stopped thinking. Could not watch any more. She knew she never had crazy thoughts, they were always flabbergastations yet, she wanted so much for this to not be a premonition. The voices started talking, as usual:

"This is about your children, the baby is your Dimitrovitch"

She did not want to hear, for some reason, something felt so terrible!

After the Olympics, one day, a voice started talking about the show. Then, the news, boom, like a thunder.

"That was Hillary Obama?"

"Hillary Obama, please tell us it is not true!"

"It is true, I ate the baby's heart, you should try it sometime, it was exhilarating!"

They were always talking about wanting Dulkinna 'to eat her heart out' she was hoping this was another hysterical outburst of the haters. Yet, the voices would not stop.

"It is true, you f..ing cow! IT WAS EXILARATING! YOU SHOULD TRY IT SOMETIME!"

"Madam, this is not true!", could you hear even the haters begging.

"What baby was that?"

"I wanted it to be mine, I wanted to eat her heart so I would become stronger at subliminal level, but they lied to me. They gave me one of hers."

"But this is cannibalism, this cannot be true!" Said again the haters.

"It's true, you f…ing imbeciles, you should try it sometime, IT WAS EXHILARATING!"

"Please stop, what to do, what to believe, God! WHAT TO DO?"

"There is nothing you can do, bitch, there is nothing you can do. It happened a few days ago!"

"Why? Could it be true? It cannot be! Could God allow such thing? Why? When will this stop? This is not true!…"

"It is true, Dulkinna, I knew about this…I was afraid to talk to you"

"Mikhail? Is that you?"

"You know it is…Please calm down, please calm down, please calm down..!"

"This is NOT TRUE!" Dulkinna shrieked out loud.

"Dulkinna, it is the true, there is nothing we can do about it any more. I had heard something about it and then I researched it in the cloud. There it is, she was biting from the baby's heart, she was in trance, like an animal!"

"This is NOT TRUE!"

"It is true, please, please calm down!"

She started eating and then went to sleep. Whenever in a state of shock like that, she immediately went into repair mode. This is how she had repaired her aneurysm after she had committed suicide. Complete detachment, ate to calm down and then went to sleep. As if she did not care, as if it happened to somebody else. Nothing else but the repetition that 'it is not true' and fell asleep. This is how she always 'repaired' herself, as if she did not care...

Over time, she found out that there is no outing. There was nobody to talk about this to at over-liminal level. No way to shout, she wanted, but the system would not allow her to cry. She even begged sometimes, but the voices announced coldly:

"If you cry, everybody on line starts crying"

"There is no point in crying any way, just calm down"

That was the life of the anchor, these were the people for which she vowed to live, to help them have a system to protect themselves from the Goulds.

Sometimes, when angry, she would shout in disbelief

"Baby eaters! Baby eaters!"

"CALM DOWN!"

CHAPTER FIFTEEN

Was 2013 A Bad Luck Year?

The Romanian harpie kept threatening with the killing of the children, for eating tomatoes (which Dulkinna learned to eat without gaining weight), for praying, for being together with her parents or with Ioobe, even for buying something nice. Dulkinna was so used to it, that she stopped believing such things can actually happen.

She first, stopped eating tomatoes, especially heirloom tomatoes. The harpie did not speak English very well and to her, those had to stand for something Dulkinna loved. Dulkinna loved her children most of all and the harpie hated her children most of all.

The harpie was a former girlfriend of Dulkinna's father and could never forgive him for marrying Adina instead of taking the harpie's hand in marriage. She boasted that she comes from the lineage of Ana from Ana and Kaiafa and ever since Lony broke up with her, she had been in the shadows, working for the Romanian Secret Services, trying to destroy the family of her former lover. She maintains that she wanted him, because she knew he was the future father of the Tsarina and she wanted herself to have been the mother.

"There was this little issue of your not being from the lineage of Virgin Mary, nothing else!" Lony once said on line.

Lony and Adina almost never came on line. They were afraid first of all of Michelle Clinton, to whom they had promised that there would be no cheating in the game. So, they could not be at subliminal level with their daughter. That was a load of bull…since they were almost constantly at under liminal level with their daughter, their only reason to continue to live on this earth. But they wanted to avoid the revenge of the haters and most of all, the harpie.

Even the harpie's sister, the mother of the prostitute, tried and compelled Lony to sleep with her in their youth. He did summon the courage to do it, but was constantly upset and thinking about his beautiful wife instead of the putrid human beeing he was sleeping with. He only did it to avoid the Securitate hurting Adina and his two children and he managed to do more wrong than good, for he enraged everybody with his afterthoughts and his remorse for having had to cheat on Adina.

The two sisters were constantly trying to kill the Tsarina, her children and just about anybody they could, from the family. Every time she bought something nice, out of sheer hatred, those two would methodically try to kill some child, in order, in their mind, to become stronger at subliminal level.

After a couple of days, Dulkinna would be told the truth on line, sometimes by them, sometimes by Mikhail, sometimes by some devotee, or some hater.

During the family vacation that Dulkinna, Ioobe and their parents took in Italy and France, hundreds and hundreds of children had been killed in Romania. Every time Dulkinna took a picture, one of her children were murdered. Some of them, who had been gathered in a military unit in Transilvania, had been assassinated with mustard gas, simply because Dulkinna looked good in a sweater of mustard color. When she returned, Dulkinna was told about it on line and she went numb, as usual. She could not believe that such things can happen in the world. She was convinced that this was the devil at work. She became more and more religious, more melancholic and less optimistic about what she could do for mankind with the system.

Ioobe could not talk to her about their children, but he was more than determined to fight for his wife's mental and physical health. He constantly tried to put on a smile for her and would call her his "sweetness". About two months after returning from Europe, he decided to take her on a trip to Hawaii. They have not been there for a while and Dulkinna just loved taking pictures in exotic places. At first she was concerned about her new weight. She was now 100 lbs overweight, not exactly prepared for a bikini vacation.

"We will go hiking, they have the most beautiful hikes through the tropical forests, we will visit botanical gardens and you will feel wonderful, you'll see."

They decided to go. She was most afraid of the plane ride there. Dulkinna could still remember the plane ride to Europe. The navy did not know how else to protect her against a plane crash, so they made the most hateful hackers and haters fly with her on the plane. Even though told that she was on the plane with them, they were so used to 'pretending', that one of the haters, destroyed the on board flying equipment of the very plane she was on, while the plane was over the Atlantic Ocean.

Dulkinna was reading her magazines and filling her Sudoku games, in order to maintain her calm. It was imperative for the anchor to maintain her calm but to not sleep on the plane. The pilot was always on the system and was not allowed to sleep on a ride with the Tsarina. It was considered too dangerous. People always did the most stupid things. So, she is always reminded that she has to be alert and very calm in order for the pilot's nervous system to be able to do the same. If she fell asleep, the pilot would have immediately fallen asleep himself.

Ioobe was sleeping and Dulkinna was fighting fatigue herself. The hacker was on board, together with his mother in law. He decided to pull one of his shenanigans. While he made the Tsarina dose off, the pilot fainted and in a heart beat, through the nervous system of the pilot, the board equipment, the entire equipment at the board of the plane went down. Then, some of the queens of Sheba on board, had called

"put the plane down" exactly at the right time.

The CIA started shouting:

"All systems up! All systems up! The Anchor's plane is in danger! Wake up, Dulkinna, be alert!"

While almost everybody on board heard the call, some of the haters were so in trance, kept by some of the haters on the ground, that they 'pretended' it was not true. Dulkinna started calling:

"I am calm, everybody, let us keep calm. Captain, this is nothing you cannot deal with! You CAN PILOT THE PLANE!"

The pilot was not answering, at subliminal level. Yet, he called at over-liminal level for:

"everybody find your seats please! It is kind of a bumpy ride and is going to be like that for a while"

"I am not giving up, I will put her plane down!" the hacker replied. And then the plane started shaking and dancing. While the pilot was trying to regain control of the plane, some people on the ground, trying to help, were trying to make the plane go in a different direction. Vladimir Putin was on line:

"Captain leave the plane do what it may! Immediately!" And the plane ride smoothed a little.

The prostitute was the one who saved the day, ironically. She went on line and could not believe that her husband, who was on the plane, had no idea that he was on the same plane with the Tsarina. They had called for more than one airplane full of people to take the trip with her and they all were pretending that she might be on a different plane. But when the plane redressed and the prostitute was admonishing her imbecile husband, everybody took notice! It was a coincidence.

"It means we are on the same plane with her!"

About at the same time, there was somewhat of an ambuscade on the plane. An old woman wanted to absolutely put the plane down. She wanted to kill herself while killing the Tsarina. The flight attendants surrounded the old lady, they started threatening her, to distract her attention and not let her focus and they called for a 'doctor'. The woman was immediately killed, on board, while the stewards and the 'doctor' were pretending she had fainted. Everybody was on line and they knew the truth at subliminal level, yet, they could not deal with it. So they pretended that:

"It cannot be true!"

The captain was constantly reassured on line that HE WILL fly the plane. Vladimir Putin, William Obama and Dulkinna, were constantly, alternatively reminding him:

"Captain, you were trained for this!"

"This is nothing you cannot deal with!"

"You can do this!"

At the same time, the prostitute was trying to keep her husband in trance and reason with him, convincing him that he is killing himself if he continues to pretend. Those, a gruesome couple of hours, Dulkinna and the captain did not dare think about anything else, but that the plane will be landed safely. Yet, the captain knew something and from time to time his mind went to it. One of the hackers on the ground, had called for "ice on the wings!". The elerons were frozen. Through a series of tricks, making the pilot focus and directing him at subliminal level to lower the altitude, the ice was melted and the captain, Dulkinna and the passengers were reassured, almost instantly. The plane took altitude again.

The landing was done manually. Dulkinna kept praying and thanking God for the daylight, of all things. She kept remembering the last plane ride of JFK JR, during the night that did not end as well as her ride.

"We could have been at the bottom of the ocean", she kept saying to herself, alternating with appreciative thoughts for a captain who landed the plane with no working radio-altimeter on board.

The captain was waiting for her at the door. They locked eyes and she said simply:

"Thank you!"

"Thank you for flying KLM, have a pleasant vacation!"

They both had tears in their eyes.

She was dreading now the ride to Hawaii. The CIA kept threatening that they will give up on her, if she ever wants to take another plane ride. The navy was preparing feverishly for her trip. They knew she will not change her mind. Almost like the hackers and the Queens of Sheba, in turn, Dulkinna would just not allow herself to be put down by the enemy. She simply kept pretending herself in turn, that this cannot happen again.

"Why do you not assassinate some of the hackers? Is the CIA out of bullets?" she blurred out.

"Forget about me, what about the other hundreds of people on board? Are you condoning home grown terrorism now?"

"The woman keeps asking for my demise!" started the hacker again.

"Shut up! We will kill you, imbecile. Those are American passengers, flying alongside her. Do you see her riding on a private plane or something? You will be judged even for what happened on the KLM flight!"

So…they prepared something else. While Dulkinna was trying desperately to keep her fears hidden even from the system, pretending to play her usual Sudoku, they put on a game…

They put her on line with her beloved son Alexander, the one without any schooling, who had dreams of becoming an architect. Mikhail had given the young man a laptop with CAD on it and Alexander mastered the program in a couple of days. He amazed the producer of the software and attracted the hate of all the hackers and of the Romanian harpie.

When Dulkinna was told that Alexander wants to make his "mother proud" she woke up with a premonition and said:

"Honey, for me, you do not have to do anything but be a happy man! And I will be most proud!"

"What made me say that?" she kept asking herself afterwards. But she gently pushed the dark thought away. She was on flight.

After the landing, she was announced that her beautiful, beloved Alexander had shot himself. He had been put in trance by the Goulds.

While Dulkinna was reassuring him, somebody else, pretending to be the Tsarina told him that he has to make a lot of money in order to please his mother. He had pulled the trigger while in trance and saying that he does not know how to please his mother any more.

She wanted to start bellowing, but could not. She felt like an animal surrounded by beasts.

"NOT ALEXANDER! NOT ALEXANDER!"

CHAPTER SIXTEEN

The Business Plan Revisited

One day, Dulkinna woke up, to hear again that the voices were agitated. The haters had a 'victory' again. They managed to determine the German military to break rank. The chancellor, was always adamant about being for over-liminality. And yet, from time to time, the voices of someone calling themselves the German people, kept asking for Dulkinna being kept at subliminal level and for her money from the game to be kept by the German government.

"There is no legal way for anybody keeping this money! The money belongs to the anchor and her children!" would always be Angela's voice shouting.

"Take your f…ing money and stop being so evil!"

"Dulkinna, you know the money belongs to you, you know you have to put your business plan into application, don't you?"

"What is her business plan?" Came a voice.

"We want the network to belong to the government" came the voice. Used to the benefits of a socialist government, the Germans kept asking their government to take care of them. The envy for the anchor's fame and possibility of becoming the richest woman in the world, after becoming over-liminal, always managed to blind them.

"Dulkinna please tell them what is your plan providing for again!" begged Angela.

"Tell them why you should be the owner of the network!" came the voice of Mikhail again.

"I shouldn't, why should I? why do I have to kill myself for these people?"

"Dulkinna!"

"Because you are an industrial nation? Because you want your engineers to be on their own free will, their spirits to not be overtaken by the Goulds and the free spirit of the creative people to be protected, while at the same time, protecting them FROM the government?"

SHE STARTED RAMBLING:

"Imagine a simple product, that some unknown thinks of. Would any government be completely free of corruption? Would that unknown be safe to pursue his dream?

What if the government flabbergasts her or him to 'forget about it' and then they pursue the invention on their own. Or what if…they decide to even kill the poor sap?"

"You need a third party owning the network. Some entity that would be kept accountable by the government and that would in turn, ensure that the government is kept accountable in the name of the people…"

"And why should that be you?"

"Because, I came up with the idea for this network, because I have the best of intentions and the integrity required and because I am the anchor. Because the system, my friends, does work with my nervous system and with my DNA"

"They want to kill you bitch, just shut up…Make her shut the f..k up!"

"Or not! You do not have to be with me. I can work with any country that does not want to be with me! We can give you the updates for the software, you can use the machine and manage your own network. How are you going to pay the network people?"

"The same way like you!"

"Do you have her creativity? Do you have her mandate even? She is the anchor! She has been kept as a slave for almost two decades. She vowed that she will not allow for anybody else to be used like this!"

"Unbelievable!"

"You want to kill her, you son of a gun?"

"We can use her foundation ourselves!..I can be the leader of the free people, why does it have to be her?" Came the voice of the hater.

"Again, do you have her pull with the people even? Does anybody give a shit about you?"

"I do not want your f..ing money! Keep the government money and show your people how you want to maintain the network yourselves!"

"Dulkinna, please stop talking like that, you know this will not happen! You cannot give up on the people, just because a couple of government employees do not wish to let go of the power they currently have over everybody!"

"How did that work for you? What is the current state of the world economy? Are you happy with the system you had? Baby eaters, this is what you all shall become! Baby eaters!"

"Dulkinna, please calm down, you do not wish to talk like that, please"

"Yes, I do! They are too evil, I should just kill myself and let you at the whim of the Goulds"

"That can be arranged bitch!"

"Shut up with the killing of oneself!"

"Why should she own the network?"

"Why should she get all the money?"

"Really? Because part of the money is hers personally from the game and no government in the world can possibly allocate money for the Goulds to feed themselves on the others!"

"Sir, Shut up!" came the hater. "I am a much better leader, I am a veritable leader, I can be the leader of the free people!"

"Only you are a Gould, you deep shit!"

"Why can't I have my own system?"

"Well do you?"

"It took ten years for us to build her system, she is the anchor! We cannot use her nervous system without bringing her over-liminal, any more!"

"We need someone with her sense of ethics and someone with her altruism even" said Mikhail.

"May we remind you people that you do have other systems, that when are used, everybody on line wants to kill or kill themselves?"

The voices would not stop rambling…Dulkinna was again into it.

"We will set up the foundation in my brother's name. The machine, for my system and the other products will be administrated by trusts within the foundation. The primary purpose of the foundation will be to allow my children to live and to build a world for them to live in."

"She only cares about her children!"

"Why does she not give us the next generation of the machine?"

"Why does her daughter not start working on the new system and the new machine?

"I want you to do everything I ask you, before I will consider doing that. I want you to respect my mother's health. That is what I asked for! I want you to respect my siblings and stop killing them by the hundreds."

"Let's just start building the new system on her DNA!"

"I will kill myself!" shouted Nadina, "you cannot force me to be an anchor!"

"The kid has to trust you, you evil people, nobody will be the anchor when you behave like that! I keep wanting to kill myself, remember? Leave my kid alone! All I asked from you was to respect my health and in return I will dedicate my life to giving you a machine and network that would ensure that everyone of you is on his own free will and that you are not left at the whim of the Goulds!"

"Why should she live in a palace like that? She will never be over-liminal! We want her dead" shouted the harpies.

"Bitch, did anybody ask what you want? Did anybody ask this harpie what she wants? I want YOU dead bitch, not her! SHE IS THE ANCHOR! Without her there is no system!"

"God, they are evil..they do not give a shit otherwise. I am the anchor. That is all I am to them! Baby eaters!" and she started praying!

"Stop praying you f..ing cow! I will kill your children! Every time you pray to God, the Romanian secret service will kill one of your children living in Romania."

"We should kill Mikhail"

"She should never have a husband like that!"

"She will never live in a palace!"

The harpies kept shrieking.

"We are queens of Sheba and we will kill you!"

"Really? Bring it on you f...ing imbecile! Kill me now! Can you?"

"Make her shut the f..K up! Bitch I am the director of the CIA, I cannot protect you from the hackers any more, shut the f..k up!...Throw the mesh over the anchor!"

The voices were now farther, like through a tunnel. She just could hear them fighting hysterically. She started eating.

"I have to calm down." And then, she went to sleep. As if, she did not care!

She woke up tired, her mind had always been working. They had been flabbergasting her all this time.

"You are not giving her her own department in the CIA. She cannot have her own navy people!"

"Who was that?"

"Michelle Clinton, madam!"

"I can't believe that bitch! What have you accomplished until now madam? Why should we continue on the same path you brought us until now? Have you destroyed the American economy?

"Don't you hear the people for which you are ready to kill yourself Dulkinna? Did you hear their shouts? All they want is your money and to kill you!"

"Not all of them"

"May I remind you that if the anchor is killed, that means an atomic war for America and whatever government whose people were guilty?" That was Vladimir Putin.

"You always keep on threatening and you only embolden them, but you are not willing to do anything else Vladimir."

"Ay, ay, ay, Dulkinna, do you not understand that I just do not know how to bring you over-liminal?"

"Dulkinna, why would you have your own people in the KGB? Or the Russian navy?"

"The same reason I have for any other country. I want to have transparency and accountability between the government and the network protecting the people. And then, even the government people need protection."

"Who will be your network made of?"

"There will be people who make an income from the network, people who pay into the network for protection and people who participate into the network simply to ensure the privacy and protection of their family, to help together with those hired and to be sure that their loved ones are on their own free will and that they are not being overtaken by the Goulds at any given time!"

"Do you understand the size of the network as you want it? This network that Mikhail created, that he says is from your idea, is a lot of work!"

"A lot of work? Then let your children be killed by the queens of Sheba. Let the creative minds and your engineers be overtaken by the hackers and the imbeciles who will steal their ideas and them maybe even kill them! You hear me? A lot of work?"

"Dulkinna calm down, please calm down! You cannot have your own department in the KGB. People are envious!"

"Not any more, Vladimir!"

"We want the anchor over-liminal, bring her home to Saint Petersburg and let us start working on rebuilding the economy and protecting our children!"

"Not all the time, madam, not all the time"

"That does not make any sense, Vladimir who are you with...?..."

"He was with the hackers from Romania"

"We will send you an atomic bomb to Bucharest! I do not care that the anchor has her family over there. You just cannot overtake the world leaders like that!"

"You will blow that bomb over your own heads, you will not bring her over-liminal. She will never live in a palace!"

"She will never receive management for that money. Some of the money should be for the Goulds!"

"Bitches, are you stupid? Who is going to give money to the Goulds to take advantage of other people?"

"We want Hillary Obama, not her, she is nothing but a cow!"

"Really? Is she now? Do you understand she is the anchor, do you understand the money is for her and her only?"

"Do you people understand that she designed this network?"

"This network is a lot of work"

"Do not break rank, whatever happens, just do not break rank!"

"Michail, I want the network to start from a hexagon around myself and I want to break that into equal triangles you should have rings of three people protecting at subliminal level at all times. For me and for you and the leaders of the world, I want the rings to work in shifts of only two hours"

"Do you realize the resources needed madam? And how are we going to pay for all of this going forward?"

"I will employ retired military people and every employer will also have its own network, that will follow my ethical standards and will exchange information with myself. They need to protect the economic and business secrets of the employer and at the same time, overview the employer and the management to not take advantage of the creatives."

"Why retired military?"

"Because they know how to follow orders!"

"Would that not make for the militarized society you are so afraid of?"

"No, because I will impose my ethics on the network. I am only trying to use people that would not become a liability for my network. Military people know how to follow orders and rules. But these people are now civilians."

"Do you understand that nobody wants to give you access to the military, nobody wants you to have all that money and all that power!"

"Then, do not give it to me! Go to Michelle Clinton and the Goulds! Eat your babies so you can become strong at subliminal level and kill people so that you could loose a couple of lbs. And find a way to pay for it all."

"Dulkinna, how are you going to pay for it?"

"For the thousand time, the trusts in the foundation, will have most of the money allocated for maintaining the network. The money from the machine, from the retail businesses I want to have and from all businesses and startups that I will form, the bulk of the money will be allocated for maintaining the network!"

"Why should we believe you?"

"Don't"

"Why should we not do it ourselves?"

"Do it! Are you?"

CHAPTER SEVENTEEN

Lisandru And Camilla

The gun that Alexander killed himself with, had been brought into the palace by a TV reporter, who gave it to Lisandru, the gipsy lover of beautiful Camilla. Apparently the TV crew…

"Only wanted to see what would happen".

While in trance, Lisandru became jealous of Alexander's intelligence. Not only was Camilla's brother, a direct son of the Tsarina and Ioobe, but he had started to receive continuous praise from Mikhail and the builder of the CAD software for his talent and ease of working with the computer program in only days.

So…he decided to give Alexander the gun…

"Not the gypsies!" Dulkinna shrieked at subliminal level. "This cannot be!"

She wanted Lisandru to leave Camilla alone.

"But they are pregnant" shouted a desperate Mikhail. "Dulkinna, he was in trance, he did not plan for this"

"No, he did not plan, but we cannot forgive everything. There have to be consequences. I do not want him with my beautiful daughter. He may remain in the palace, but has to ponder on the actions that brought him here."

"I do not want him anymore! I will have an abortion" shouted Camilla.

"Honney, do not do that! Listen to your mother! We will raise the child. You will end up being sorry if you kill the baby! Listen to me!"

After a couple of days, Lisandru killed himself. The gun had been brought into the palace by another TV crew member. Camilla kept asking for an abortion. Mikhail and Dulkinna tried to no avail to make her change her mind.

"This was a child that came out of love, it is a beautiful soul that answered the call. Do not kill it, Camila. We will raise him as our own, should you not wish to! Do not make the mistake your mother had made as a teenager"

Immediately after the abortion, Camila started regretting it. She now, wanted the child, to remember Lisandru by.

"Why God?" Dulkinna sighed… "that is all I am always asking for: do not forsake my children and deliver them from the devil. Why?"

"Where is your God now, cow?"

"You hear Dulkinna?"

"These are the stupids you want to work with, for them you are dedicating your life, are you not?"

"These are some of the stupids, madam. Not everybody is as evil as you are!"

"You f…ing cow!"

"Behold Satan!" she started shouting out loud. "I cannot deal with this, I cannot deal with this!"

She felt the mesh being thrown over her. The navy must have taken charge…She ate and went to sleep.

Beautiful Camilla was the surrogate granddaughter of the gypsy who had been raising the Tsarina for a short time, when a child. The beautiful Ilinca, had loved the Tsarina, her mother, father, her little brother, but most of all, she was admiring the Tsarina's grandmother. She had raised Camilla and another younger daughter, Alexandra, natural child of Dulkinna and Ioobe, as the Tsarina had been raised by her grandmother, madam Avram.

Camilla, now a teenager, had Alexandra, a toddler, in her care. She had developed her maternal instincts early, while taking care of the sibling. She liked fashion, she wanted a child, she wanted to study, she wanted to become rich on her own, to have her own business, like her brother Alexander started having,…She was a wonderful, wonderful teenage daughter, that gave back to the Tsarina the will to live.

"It is not easy to be with so many of them without you", Mikhail would complain.

"I know that, my love, but just remember that: I envy YOU! When it is hard, just think of me and Ioobe, what we have to put up with and how you are our only hope. I remember you and the children, this is how I always resolve to go on living. You do the same. Please, do the same!"

"We want you, we just want to be with you, mother!"

"I know Camilla, we will be together…but if…"

"Mother stop that, we cannot deal with that, you cannot prepare us for the eventuality of your demise any more. We cannot deal with that! We want you, we need you here with us!"

Dulkinna started again reminiscing about the 'explosion'. She was in disbelief again, ready to deny that the children even existed… "Not again!"…She pushed that thought away.

At the beginning of 2013, she went to the dentist to have a crown installed on a molar. The Navy and the CIA kept begging her to resist the dentist and to not have it done, but never explained anything else. She was always getting angry when feeling people getting evil and usually became carelessly mad.

The doctor, supposedly was preparing to install a vile with cyanide in her molar. She did not care.

"You have one anchor to protect" she would shout at the navy people. "I do not care, I just do not care any more"

She came home with extreme pain. The doctor had managed to cut her jaw with the syringe needle, by injecting her several times with Novocain one injection after another almost in the same place. When asked why the pain, the doctor responded that the crown takes some getting used to. So..she waited.

After about a month, she went to the doctor, complaining of ear infection, while the doctor delivered the bad news.

"There is nothing wrong with your ear, your jaw is broken and the jaw joint is swollen; Hence the strong pain."

"What can we do for this?"

"Nothing, you cannot chew…for about six months…until it starts healing."

Then, the hackers announced that the Tsarina will finally be killed.

"The doctor installed a vile with TNT into your molar, bitch."

"You will explode you f…ing cow!"

She could not believe this. Apparently it had been the order of Michelle Clinton. She wanted the Tsarina dead and while the people would go hysterical in the absence of the machine, Michelle Clinton would emerge as the mother bringing the nation back together and finally win her coveted presidential election.

The people could see on the system the vial with TNT, being dissolved steadily, by the Tsarina's nervous system, when the tought was flabbergasted.

Dulkinna was incredulous.

"How could this be? Who has ever heard such a thing?"

"It is true Dulkinna, we can see the vial dissolving.."

"We will take you over-liminal and extract the tooth" Vladimir would promise.

Until, in January 2014, the Tsarina came to the realization that she has to do something about it herself.

"I will go to the dentist and request to have the tooth extracted through surgery, on grounds that the jaw is broken and he should not hurt the jaw"

While reassuring her that the doctor is waiting for her and will do the surgery, the navy was fighting with the demons. They had announced her that she had literally days remaining until the explosion. She started praying for it to happen when Ioobe was not home and begged the neighbors to leave their homes during that week.

When she arrived at the surgeon's office, she was told, that she should wait her turn, as the doctor did not have time to extract the tooth. She could not believe her ears. She thought doctors were afraid to perform the terrifying surgery. In reality, the whole world was keeping vigil and waiting for her demise.

On the day of January 7th, Mikhail and the children were holding candles and decided for telling her that she will undoubtedly explode.

She ate and went to sleep…

When she woke up, the hysteria had again started…the vial had dissolved and that it had been no explosion. The CIA was triumphant.

"Yes! We did this!"

Hillary Obama's man, who was in charge with giving the dentist the vial with TNT, switched it with one with Novocain instead. She dodged the bullet again…Again, she wished she had died instead…

"What about us, mother?"

CHAPTER EIGHTEEN

The Network Has Its Limitations

"Do you realize, that she is pretending…"

"Bitch, shut the f..k up! Everybody, everybody knows what you are trying to say and do. You want to program us at subliminal level? Do you realize that we know what you have at under-liminal, at subliminal and at over-liminal level?"

"How the f..k do they know that again?"

"All I wanted to say was that…"

"Bitch, do you understand that not only is this machine working for you to try and program people at subliminal level, but we also can see everything you want to do? Also, do you realize that this woman could never pretend? We know everything this woman has done since she was traveling through the birth canal. Do you get that?"

"William Obama! William Obama! William Obama!"

"What bitch? What? Do you realize who I am? Do you realize that I am the most powerful man in the world? You shout my name and I am supposed to come on line?"

"Sir, I do not want her pretending…"

"Bitch, did I just tell you something? Did I just tell you something? How dare you?"

"I will never allow her to become over-liminal! I do not want her."

"Has anybody asked the f..ing prostitute what she wants? I am William Obama and I want to know! Have you checked with the f..ing prostitute to see what she wants? Has anybody asked you madam? You want to keep me in trance? You want to keep me in trance? How stupid are you bitch?"

"Kill the f..ing imbeciles!"

"Really, Hillary Obama?"

"Did I ever betray you madam, the way you betrayed me just now?"

"Who the f…k do you think you are?"

"I am somebody who will never take no for an answer. This is who the f..k I am and I want to be the leader of the free people!"

"But you are a Goauld" came the sarcastic answer.

"So what if I am? So what If I am?"

"Thank You Jesus, thank You Lord!" Dulkinna was laughing out loud.

"Not again, madam! Why do you keep taking the Lord's name in vain Dulkinna?"

"Because God works in mysterious ways and the devil keeps showing us how stupid he is."

"Mother f..er, Mother f…er!"

"Yeah! What the f..k can I tell you?"

Conversations like these were almost a constant on the line. When she could not take it any more, Dulkinna would crash glasses or break her china. This was a way to make noise so that everybody who heard it would get on line and stop the haters and hackers from cussing and cursing at her incessantly.

Another terrorizing strategy was to pretend to be Mikhail or somebody Dulkinna trusted, to try and get close to her at subliminal level and then hurt her. She was usually the only one who knew who these people were, so she would tell them:

"Yeah, sure you're Mikhail, you are not the hacker at all!"

"How the f…k did she know?"

"I am the central nervous system of the machine, imbecile, when you logged in your computer, you gave your name. Your computer is flabbergasting my nervous system and, by the way, I can hear your real voice too. At subliminal level you are not imitating anybody."

Yet, if the mesh was on, or if they tried to communicate at under-liminal level, it was hard for the Anchor to figure out who they were. So, she would start cussing at them, or offend them in any matter and their nervous system would give in, usually in a matter of seconds, they started cussing or cursing at her at subliminal level and then she knew who they were.

We have to do something about the technology. The machine should identify these people even when they are at under-liminal level. Also, when they come hovering, with the power of their minds, without using the machine. We have to do something about that. Dulkinna was making mental notes.

"I am here Dulkinna, I am taking notes." Mikhail would invariably say.

"I am Bill Gates, Dulkinna, if we use the handshake protocol between the computers, on the network that Mikhail designed, we can always know the whole truth, only it will be found out after the fact."

"That is OK", said Nadina. "I wrote a piece of code that would ensure that we know the truth even for those who were not on line, after they get on line and log into their computers. If they try to hurt somebody, at subliminal level, with the power of their mind, we will know everything about it, once they use their smart phone even."

"Who the f..k do you think you are? Let's kill her!"

"We'll kill you, you son of a gun, we'll kill you! Nobody wants to be programmed by the hackers. Nobody wants to be taken over by the Goulds. Even the Goulds want to know who is trying to overtake them!"

"What the f…k is she pretending? Bitch, do you understand, that I am Hillary Obama and I am telling you.."

"You are not the hacker are you?"

"Oh f..k you! I am the prostitute, how dare she? How the f…k did she know this?"

"You were trying to pretend to be the hacker pretending to be Hillary Obama, weren't you madam?"

"How dares she pretend this?"

"What the f..k is she pretending you f...ing criminal? Do you understand bitch that NOW, I know everything you are thinking? How the f...k can you intend to overtake me while I am aware of you?"

"Mr. President, I f...ed with you, how can you tell me that she should not be killed?"

"Because not everybody, but everybody needs the Anchor, you f...ing imbecile! Nobody needs you. Do you understand that you are not even good in bed, you f..ing cow? Do you understand that only Hillary Obama wants me to sleep with you, to spice up the relationship? How the f..k dare you talk to me about such things on line?"

"Who the f...k do you think you are whiteie?"

"This is not true, this is not true" the prostitute started repeating to herself, as not to hurt herself at subliminal level.

"What the f...k am I going to do?"

"Dulkinna...Dulkinna please do not hurt your head! Please calm down!"

"Madam, calm down immediately! Throw the mesh, throw the mess, order her to calm down! Protect the Anchor!"

"How am I going to deal with this? What will I end up doing for these people? I cannot take this anymore!" The Anchor was rambling.

"Stop saying that! Or I will kill myself, do you hear me Dulkinna? Madam, I need to know if you heard me!"

The communication was difficult because of the mesh. The electronic mesh they threw over the Tsarina in such situations, determined everybody to be distanced from the Tsarina. This time however, they seemed like talking from out of space.

"This is a gift from Mark Zuckerberg, do you understand madam?" came the big inventor's explanation out of nowhere. "I have written a piece of code that will absolutely throw them into space when the mesh is over you! This is my contribution at protecting the Anchor!"

"Dulkinna, do you understand that the people had broken rank? I cannot deal with this! How can this happen?"

"Mikhail, please calm down, please remember me, as I remember about you and the children!"

"Do you understand that I cannot deal with this?"

"what are you telling…Mikhail, who are you with? My system, what is going on? Who betrayed Mikhail this time?"

"Nobody, madam! Nothing is going on! He was with the hacker!"

"Why don't you protect him?"

"Because we have no way of knowing it, until after the fact, madam. The hacker was not on the system. He used the power of his mind."

"Mikhail, are you OK? Every time you have a weird thought like that, please remember to ask the system what is going on!"

"Do you understand that we are the navy and had done that ourselves? He will be OK. Please calm down! We asked the question!"

"I want him to ask the question! I want him to become aware, as to not ever hurt himself!"

"Nobody is aware, madam. When you are overtaken, even you do not know!"

"I know that, but I become aware faster than all of you on line."

"Do you understand, madam, that I will never give up? I will never give up trying to kill you!"

"You son of a gun, WE will kill you! Nobody needs a hacker, nobody!"

"Really? Are there no bullets any more? Why are you reasoning with the hacker? Why?"

"Calm down! Just calm her the f..k down! Shut up bitch, this is the director of the CIA. Shut the f…k up!"

"It is the FBI, madam, they do not want to start killing American citizens. We are afraid that if we start, we will never stop the killing."

"Are you shitting me? Are you shitting me? What about us, normal citizens? Why do we have to put up with this?"

"It's her, you should kill her!"

"Bitch, do you understand that we will kill you and not her? Do you understand that nobody needs another stupid, but everybody needs the anchor?"

"Why the f…k should she be allowed to live? When I cannot deal with my cancer? Do you understand that my cancer returned? Why should she be allowed to repair herself when we cannot heal ourselves like her?"

"You hear them, these are the stupids! This is who you want to kill yourself for!"

"Yes, madam Hillary Obama, it is because you have confused them to such a degree and because they cannot deal with the reality any more! Do you people realize that you are living in a make believe world, while I am the only human being who knows her own reality? How can you people pretend to such a degree? How can you want me dead madam?"

"I am pretending that if I want you dead, I will be stronger at subliminal level! I only wanted you dead, that is all!"

"That is ALL? Nothing else! Nothing else…."

It was time for her to eat and go to sleep…..

CHAPTER NINETEEN

Maria

"Maria, what happened?"

"Nothing mother. Nothing."

"Maria does not want to leave any more, but nothing happened."

"Maria, what is wrong honey? While I was asleep I could hear that you tried to kill yourself? What is wrong?"

"I am fine now! I just was thinking again that I would have liked to have a husband of my own by now…."

"A husband and a child or your own…you will have them, I promise you."

"why would I bring another child into this world?"

"Honey, remember how I many times ask God why did my parents ever conceive my brother and I, in front of such adversities? It is because you have to live your life believing in God. You cannot submit to the devil's wishes and become afraid. God is always with you, as my father keeps telling me and you just live your life and trust in God's Great Plan. You have to have your child and then you pour your heart out for that child. This is what life is all about, this is what our time here on earth is for. For things like that, for fighting the fight and for pretending that the devil and the evil doers will never prevail…"

Dealing with life

Dealing with a life like ours
Is never easy, what do I say
When it does not rain it pours!
But now if I may:
Does anyone have access
To such reason for treason?
Was anyone ever betrayed
Have their spirits in such ways been swayed?
We have each other,
And what else?
How can this be? Why so intense?
Why should we continue
To pretend to be such an ingenue?
You've burned us and now we know how
To throw away your pretense, we will not bow!
We will not allow for your vile,
You cannot defy us with that putrid smile.
You overtook my child, you made us run wild,
Now, we know for sure, what lies
Underneath your putrid, stinking smiles.
We won't give up on each other,
Instead, we will fight and then bother
To look back! Watch out fool!
There will be nothing left, when we pool
Our hatred for your disdain,
You make us laugh, still looking for gain?
'you fooled me twice, shame on me,
You tried again, I've let you be,
But now, the fourth, it is our turn
To bring despair, your life to churn!'
From down here, now it seems
You want my friendship, you send beams,
You think a fool have I become,

I may look like that to some,
But I am not, I do assure,
I see treason in your demure,
I see the vile in your smile.
I love my child, you will not win,
Our regard for you did dim
The light in our eyes is bright,
And there is more wise in our disguise!
I love my child and I resolve
For your despair, I will be bold!
Towards your misery I will sing,
And YOUR demise I will bring!
My child will dance, the dance of life
My child will sing and she will strife,
I'll shut YOUR mouth and in that shot,

I will resolve to not forget,
How vile you were and desuet!
You've sent us weapons grade desease
You've sent us viles with TNT and THIS,
Is you want us to forget? Never again, my dear 'friend'!
Reality with pain you have infused,
And now you wish I were confused?
You wish my love, lack of refrain,
Because you cannot deal with pain?
Be it cold or way too hot,
But scorn for you is all I've got!
I may be shrude, I may be cruel,
Never again I'll be your fool!

Maria was the natural daughter of Dulkinna and Ioobe. The surrogate mother who gave birth to her, was a medical doctor from Romania, who met the Tsarina on a trip to Paris. She knew about Ioobe, the Tsarina's boyfriend at the time. She knew he was a man of higher intelligence, yet she was convinced the Tsarina must have been a woman of below average IQ. Otherwise, how could she have been a cow and have no idea whom she was supposed to be, when everybody around her was gossiping only about this? She must have been a stupid, un-capable to communicate at subliminal level. She knew about the Tsarina having been flabbergasted to have an abortion and she knew that Dulkinna was un-aware of what flabbergasting was, at that time. She also knew that the doctor who 'saved her life', had done so only after harvesting her eggs. She decided to have a baby of the Tsarina, the supposed messenger of God and the wonderfully intelligent and handsome young man who was preparing to become the Tarina's husband. Yet, she wanted the child to look only as Ioobe. She did not know yet if she ever would tell the truth to the progenitor.

Maria had told her natural mother that she looked exactly like Ioobe's aunt and his cousin. She was 27 years old when she contacted the Tsarina at subliminal level and she was a Sociology PhD student at Harvard. She was already proud to tell her mother that she was a published author and that she had just to finish her thesis and would obtain her coveted Harvard diploma. For now, though, she wanted to see her mother over-liminal.

She decided to dedicate her life to studying the mother she never knew enough about, even though she thought she knew everything. Nobody was more happy than Maria, when they allowed the Tsarina to go at subliminal level, when they started giving her confirmations and figured out that in fact, she was the best subliminal communicator in the world. They could not understand for a while, why the Tsarina could not have under-liminal conversations. Then, after a series of discussions, they figured out that it was the fault of the technology that was linked to her DNA. Dulkinna did not have the luxuries of other superior minds. She understood what was told to her at under-liminal level, but she could not answer back without bringing the information subliminal or even over-liminal, This was because of all the flabbergasting. Everybody on line wanted to know what was she doing, what was she trying to say and sometimes the hackers brought even her own thoughts at over-liminal level, before she could realize she was thinking them. The process was hurting her nervous system and everybody shouted at the hackers to cut it out nowadays. Never the less, the system was constantly bombarded with inquiries about what was she trying to say. People wanted to know what she had to say about something, if possible, before Dulkinna did.

When she found out that Mikhail had indeed started to talk to the Tsarina at subliminal level, she decided to meet him. She wanted to know if he was indeed in love with her mother, like everybody else did, but more than that, she wanted to ask him how dare he ignore the fact that the Tsarina was still married to Maria's father, Ioobe and that they had the most happy marriage in the world?

One day, Maria went to a basketball game of the Brooklyn Nets and arranged to brush shoulders with the owner of the team while whispering:

"I am her natural daughter!"

"Please stay away from me", the answer came from a frightened Prokhorov, who was wondering if anybody had noticed the beautiful young woman and her foolish gesture.

After he started gathering the children in the Petersburg palace, he contacted Maria himself and invited her there. She had started conversations with the Tsarina at subliminal level and revealed herself as a daughter to the haters. He was trying to protect every natural child of the Tsarina.

Due to her expertise in human behavior and sociology, both Mikhail and Dulkinna deferred to Maria many times to figure out what was happening on the network. She was very much trusted and yet, she still could not accept Mikhail's daring intentions of asking the Tsarina to divorce Ioobe and give him 'his turn at fulfilling his destiny'.

More than anything else, Maria hated Mikhail for his constant partying with beautiful women, who constantly wanted to marry him and who were killing the children and even trying to kill the husband to be, out of jealousy.

The elderly gypsy lady who was trying to keep the gypsies in the compound happy and together, in order to raise the toddlers and babies living there, had the same thoughts. A hidden woman, she was posing as a child lover, but all she could think about was that the gypsies were supposed to roam the streets begging and that the children would have been better of into the world than gathered in that beautiful palace where they did not belong. After all, most of them had been raised as gypsies, by the gypsies, with no formal education. This is how these children managed to survive the wrath of the Romanian harpie and the haters.

Unhappy, disappointed, overwhelmed by the sheer number of siblings in the compound, missing her work at Harvard, Maria did not realize that she was overtaken. She thought everything had a logic and that her growing hate for Mikhail, the man who had given her a home and entrusted her with so much, was genuine.

One evening, while having supper together, as usual, Maria slipped him a pill given by the old gypsy.

"This will teach him to sleep with all those women!" the gypsy said.

After supper, Mikhail became violently ill and Maria could not think of anything else but that she should now, kill herself. Michelle Clinton advised on line, that he had been given weapons grade STD, through a pill sent by herself and slipped into his food by the beloved daughter. While Mikhail was in pain and desperate, he felt the most hateful, disappointed thoughts for Maria and the young woman was trying desperately to end her life. Yet, in a moment of lucidity, he called for the Tsarina. He feared that the child might actually kill herself. This is what Dulkinna woke up to that night.

"What is happening, my system who is Maria with? Who has betrayed Mikhail? Vladimir Putin come on line! My system what is going on?" came the desperate cries of the Tsarina, instantly.

"They were with the hackers!" came the answer from the navy.

"Please calm down! We will send you the antidote"

"Don't worry, we are the KGB, do you think we will allow him to take another one of your pills? We have your own antidote."

"This is weapons grade Gonorea, are you sure you have the antidote for it? He should start taking it immediately. He might loose his hair. It is a powerful antibiotic."

"Not my hair", was lamenting Mikhail and Dulkinna started an almost smile.

"Dulkinna, how could you smile woman? You love my hair."

"I just felt you, Mikhail, we were in direct contact for a fraction of a second. I felt you."

"Oh God, that is true! God how I wish I were in direct contact with your DNA now!"

"Are you stupid?" Came the shout from Hillary Obama:

"You cannot seriously want that now, that the hackers are all on the prowl. Protect the Tsarina! Throw the mesh!"

"Oh, God!"

"Mikhail, what is going on?"

"I will have to kill myself now. I cannot be allowed to be near you now woman. They have finished me!"

"Mikhail! Mikhail! I had enough of this! Calm down. You shall calm down, take the antidote and start the process of repairing yourself. Do you hear me? No more nonsense about killing oneself from anyone of you!"

"Look at that Michelle Clinton! She is livid. Do you want to give her the satisfaction? Take the f..ing antidote, for God's sake. You will not lose your hair. Just take the medication and calm down!" came the voice of Vladimir Putin.

"What are we going to do, woman, what are we going to do? You are the messenger of God!"

"Yeah, the messenger that had an abortion, remember? And who is supposed to divorce the first husband and marry the husband to be... Enough of your low self-esteem. Repair yourself!" Dulkinna ordered.

"Just do not toss me to the side, Dulkinna, I am nothing if I am not your husband to be..."

"Enough, enough of this! Repair mode, repair mode. You calm down and order your system to repair itself."

"How do you want me to do that?"

"You start with complete detachment. You calm yourself down immediately! Remember the game when you were supposed to have AIDS? Have I given up on you then?"

"No and I thought you were a total imbecile for it!"

"That is because you knew it was a lie, but I did not. I will never give up on you! Not now, when you have started taking care of the children, not ever. Think of your destiny, Mikhail, have you fulfilled it? Can you afford to die now?"

"Oh God, this is God's wrath Dulkinna, for all those times when I went to your home and never did ring the bell. We should have been over-liminal by now! This is God's wrath!"

"Pray, pray! Enough lament."

"What do you want me to do mother?"

"Maria, calm down, I do not have time for your trying to kill yourself now. Please ask the system who you are with!"

"She is with the hacker, mother, we know it, but she does not want to believe us. We will keep vigil and she will be on suicide watch." Shouted the scared voice of a son.

"Dulkina, I would like to talk to you about your third poetry book. You promised me that you will write a dedication for it" Asked Mikhail.

"Yes, I have to write something for Lessons for a new generation. I want to dedicate it to all our children."

"You still do not want to publish it yourself?"

"No, I prefer for you to publish it before I come over-liminal, I will send you the dedication…"

………………………………..

I dedicate this book to all our children, those living in Saint Petersburg and also to those from all around the world, still waiting to meet their natural parents. I love you each as if you were the only one….

CHAPTER TWENTY

The Children Vow To Never Again Give Up On Each Other

We'll never give up on each other!
Remember this from your wife and mother.
Through sickness and health we will strife,
To our enemies chagrin, we'll survive.
Can we still bring each other love?
Can we laugh at what we've got?
Can we cry together when it is not better?
Can we remember? Can we forgive?
Then we'll be proud and God! Shall we LIVE!
We can be tough, we can smile,
We can still bring each other flowers at life's trial,
We can keep each other warm and protect from scorn,
We must remember the future, never forget the past,
And we'll keep on seeing the light at last!
Our love will survive, like a young lioness

I find sweetness and warmth in our togetherness,
My roar you will seek, yours I embrace
When I hunt with you, I smell every trace,
Like the cubs seeking milk,

Each other we feel, we seek and we find,
That happiness was always near and kind!
With you, love and life go hand in hand,
I'll never give up singing in your band.
Your tune and the tone, I will seek forever,
Whatever may come, we will be together.
We'll never give up on each other,
Remember this, from your wife and your mother!

While Dulkinna was writing this message for her children, they started calling to her and promising that they will never break rank. The network will start being better prepared for he hacker's attacks.

"I want you on two hours shifts at the most, during the night. This way you will not grow tired or bored and if you are overtaken by the hackers, you will soon be changed by somebody else who will start keeping vigil. Any weird thought will immediately be reported to those around you. You cannot think about suicide. That is a sin!"

"What about you mother? What about your constant threats of suicide? Is that not a sin?"

"Of course it is, I am only trying to keep myself alive though, am I not? Whenever I make a threat like that, it is because I wish to take it out of my system. Because I wish to remind myself that I still have you. You are my only reason to live!"

"But, that is blasphemy, mother, don't you understand that yourself?"

"You are right about it and yet, when I see the people's hatred and evilness I become enraged and I am overwhelmed with the desire to remove the anchor from them. But then, I remember you and I do not wish to leave you in such world do I not? Would you kindly remember me? I only live for you all! Please no more threats of suicide, the trace of a thought is going to be reported to myself or Mikhail and to the loved ones around you."

"We will never give up on Mikhail or each other again, mother, even the gypsies have resolved that we will live together as a family. There are 500 more gypsies who are expected into the compound, including the natural children and their surrogate families."

"The second palace is now complete, Dulkinna. We will start working on the Industrial building, the one resembling a casino building. I have to get the permits."

"I do not want such a building in San Petersburg, it shall be a lower rise, shouted Vladimir"

"I want us to live as decent people, Dulkinna, I thought of what you said, about having penthouses for them. I wish you were here…"

"You did good, Mikhail, remember we thought that there are only 250 children and that seemed like a lot, did it not?"

"We are now 1100 people in the two palaces, Dulkinna. We are expecting another 500."

"That is just too many…"

"Who was that? Who dared say that? Which one of the children is too many? Who dared say that?"

"It was the old gypsy mother."

"I am overwhelmed, that is all!"

"Please madam, I am forever grateful to the gypsies for bringing my children into this world and for raising them as my grandmother had raised me, with love, love and understanding. But these are my children. You have to understand that we cannot turn back time. The gypsies who have my children are now hunted down everywhere, by the haters and the hackers. They are overtaken and now, they need protection themselves. I have begged for your help, but not for this!"

"I am sorry Dulkinna, I was overtaken, I must have been overtaken!"

"Madam, from now on, you will live in the villa, you cannot be in the palace with the children!"

"But, Mikhail, why don't you send her home?"

"I need all the help I can get, Dulkinna. The gypsies are envious of each other. They come here with the best of intentions, but then they want their children to be my favorite and things like that. I cannot take it anymore!"

"Enough, not again. Think of myself! Can I still take it? What do you think?"

"We need to start the industrial building and I have no liquidity for it. I need cash!"

"I collected $4 billion in proceeds from your novel and that is not enough. My assets are all tied up."

"Why don't you ask Dmitry for funds from the game?"

"I do not want us to become over-liminal and for them to say that the funds have been mismanaged...Dmitry happens to agree."

"We will have to find something to do...what about jewelry?" said Dulkinna who was browsing through a magazine, while having the conversation.

"Dulkinna, jewelry does not bring as much money as you think, it is always owned by at least three or four governments and those funds cannot be touched under over-liminality"

"No, I am not thinking of the game. I am thinking of your diamond mines and about your going into the jewelry business. I could design some jewelry and the devotees would purchase it. This would not be jewelry that I purchase, I would not even have access to it. In fact, it could not even be in the game. But the devotees would buy it, to help you and the children, just like they buy all the things in the game."

"Dulkinna, they buy the things in the game, because they have the opportunity to win the lotteries, they will not buy my jewelry and I cannot go for jewelry."

"Why not?"

"I cannot go for that...I am not in the jewelry business,...people are envious..."

"Well, suit yourself! How do you want me to help? You want me to go into nickel now?"

"Dulkinna, I did not mean that, why do you snap? I just do not know how to do this...people want to destroy me, not to buy my jewelry?"

"Really, do you know many authors who earned $4 billion with one novel? Is that even true? That is unheard of. And I did not receive any earnings report whatsoever..."

"Please stop that. It is absolutely the truth. Everybody wanted to read what you have to say...I told you, the editor thought it was too much money, that would bring you over-liminal and decided to pretend that you are in the game..."

"I am in the game, but the contract for publishing was an over-liminal contract…."

"Are you asking me about what is going on in America? I have not even been in that country in months. You have asked me to stay with the children and this is what I am doing. I am not letting anything happen to them again…I have to find a way to bring you over-liminal though…"

"So, no jewelry project"

"why jewelry, do you understand it does not bring that much money?"

"But this would bring you the full proceeds, not just 1% of sales. You would be the over-liminal owner of the company and people would simply buy it because they would know that I designed it."

"I do not know, I do not think so…"

"Just think about it."

"Enough about the jewelry, there will be no jewelry, I do not want you telling me what to do!"

????????????

"Oh, God, he is with the hacker."

"God I am sorry, Dulkinna, please forgive me, you know I do not talk like that to you when I am myself."

"Suit yourself, I was only trying to help, but you don't want it, I am disconsolate and dismayed" she humored him.

CHAPTER TWENTY ONE

The Plans For An Industrial Building, A Clubhouse And The Parks

"Dulkinna, wake up, please wake up, I am with you and I want us to talk."

"OK, what is going on?"

"We are overcrowded, we sleep almost four people in a bedroom, it is almost un-hygienic"

"You should build an industrial building, Mikhail, you should have it built by a company that specializes in casinos"

"Casino? Why a casino? You should see these two buildings Dulkinna, they are full of character, these are palaces. Why build a casino?"

"I want you to have that open space at the ground floor, for a dining room. Think about it, for a wedding or for the birthday cakes every weekend, you will have to fit almost 5000 people in there, only with us and the children. When you count the gypsies and their families, you really need the space"

"Not an industrial building! It does not fit with the other two, these are four level buildings, Dulkinna"

"Make the industrial one a five or six level building. I want it to have only penthouses at the upper levels. You want three or four bedroom apartments for the gypsies to live in, with our children, for their extended families and even for our grown up children and their families."

"We need some parking space."

"Have it underground of the industrial building…have you started having the birthday cakes yet?"

"Those always get postponed"

"Yes, mother, he is always busy, but we started having them"

"But I asked you to have them with Mikhail. They have to feel that you are paying interest Mikhail, they have to feel that you love them all, not just Alexandra and Camilla."

"I do pay attention Dulkinna, I just did not have time, that is all"

"I want every week, those who celebrate their birthday, to prepare something about themselves to say. They have to present it to you, or to give it to you to present it to the others. This way you will learn their names faster and even things about them, they will feel more loved and you will become a family easier and faster."

!!!!!!!!!!!

"Mikhail, you do not want to do that?"

'It is not that I do not want, I do pay attention. Whenever somebody comes into the compound I take a saliva swab and I do their DNA myself. I know which are your children with me, with Ioobe, which are mine with other women or Ioobe's with other women…we have even grandchildren already. But they are envious Dulkinna, I cannot deal with this! It is too much. I cannot deal with our children being envious and even hating each other"

"We are too many here!"

"I will not hear that, do you hear me? Do you see me being a prisoner here? Think about all your siblings that were murdered! I will not hear that! I will not hear that! I am your mother and I love every one of you! Which one of you is too many, honey? How can we talk like that?"

"That is because he was overtaken by the gypsy lady!"

"which one? why? How can this happen? They must have been overtaken by the Romanian secret service again!"

"I am your son and you go right by me and do not even know that I exist!"

"I do not? You have a son, don't you, our first grandchild, you are my son with the Tsarina. Do I know? Do I know? Did I do your DNA when you came into the palace? How can you believe that I do not know you? I cannot know every one of you, but I try!"

"Where are they coming from?"

"Macedonia, Dulkinna, they really do not want you there, madam."

"Have you been schooled honey?"

"I am a schoolteacher!"

"I want you to school the young ones. In the industrial building, you will have some conference rooms and you will start home schooling the young ones. This son of ours can be in charge of that project"

"No schooling for these children, they will not be schooled, Dulkinna, I do not want any more of them to be murdered or overtaken and made to kill themselves because of their superior intelligence!"

"Michail, what are you talking about? We will not give up in face of adversity! They want to study. These are our children, they have creative minds, you cannot keep them stifled like that."

"What is the purpose, not now, Dulkinna, not now! I cannot deal with another suicide! I really cannot deal any more."

"From now on, I want every dark thought reported to Mikhail! I cannot emphasize that enough! You do not go to the gypsy lady, you go to Mikhail! And you tell him what came over you! Mikhail, they also have to learn to ask immediately: My system what is wrong with me? My system what is going on? Who is doing this to me?"

"That is easier said than done, Dulkinna. Usually they think they have a reason for thinking what they are thinking. The hackers are not stupid. They put a reason at under-liminal level even. We do not have any idea what came over us."

"You are the only one mother, only you are aware when you are overtaken by the hackers or the secret service."

"Every time you think something weird, something against one of the siblings, against Mikhail or against the gypsies or your mother, you will ask the system, what is wrong with me?"

"How do you know it mother?"

"Well, usually I put two and two together! I figure out when a thought is out of place. When I do not feel that it belongs, when it does not characterize me. Let us take the feeling that Mikhail does not care. How could that be? He puts himself out there, spends billions of euros to build you a home, to put a roof over your head, to take care of all of you. He is trying to gather all of you, bring all of you home to Russia and why would you think he does not care? When you have a thought like that, it is time to ask the system: What is wrong, who am I with?"

"But mother, I thought he does not care, he passes me by on the hallway and does not say anything!"

"Do you realize how many of you are here? How could I not care? I cannot deal with this Dulkinna, I cannot deal with this!"

"Mikhail, what is wrong, who are you with?"

"He is with the hackers"

"I hate these people! They will have to be eliminated! These are people that cannot let other people live! Vladimir, you are killing my children!"

"Ay, ay, ay, Dulkinna, what makes you think I do not want to take you over-liminal? But not right now, not right now! I just do not know how to do it!"

"Are my children in Russia? Talk about them on a press conference."

"Don't you understand that your husband to be put them on TV? And they started being flabbergasted, they started killing themselves. It was the TV crew that smuggled the gun with which Alex and Lisandru killed themselves into the compound, remember?"

"Just bring them over-liminal, I want them on the first page of the newspapers, talk about them. My children exist do they not? Is this man still a play boy billionaire? He has created a home for 1100 children and gypsies. Is that not newsworthy? I want to read that in the news!"

"Not right now, Dulkinna, not right now!"

"Mother please stop doubting that we exist, I am Nadina, I can feel you! I do exist! I cannot deal with this! I do exist mother, I am in San Petersburg and I do exist!"

"I am sorry, from time to time, my system needs a reality check that is all!"

"How can she have 1100 children?"

??????????

"Dulkinna not you too, they took the eggs when you had your abortion in Romania, remember? Why are you doing this? It is hurting all of us at subliminal level, we cannot deal with your feeling like this!"

"I am sorry honey, I just am overwhelmed from time to time, that is all! I was just wondering how is that possible for them to have so many eggs that is all!"

"We know that, you had that at subliminal level. Some of the children are mine with various women or Ioobe's with different women, remember?"

"Yes, but then, some of them are mine with other men!"

"They took your eggs every time you went to the gynecologist Dulkinna."

"Every time you wished to have a baby, they created one in a peatreedish"

"But then why kill them?"

"The harpie from the Romanian Secret Service only brought them into this world in order to sacrifice them to the devil, Dulkinna, remember that??"

"God, I cannot believe this, let me pray…please let me pray…Our Heavenly Father……God protect and save our children, keep them into your care,…. enlighten them and lit their path…"

"God how this woman is praying, how can you still believe in God like that madam?"

"…God forgive me, save me, protect and deliver me from evil, Amen!"

"Please allow me to pray, I need to do that, I cannot deal with anything anymore!"

"Let her pray, let her pray! Came the voice of the Romanian harpie."

Dulkinna had stopped; From time to time, she just stopped thinking. The voices were curious, they started asking: "How can she not have anything not even at under-liminal level? How can she not think of anything? Nobody else does that!"

"Mikhail, about the compound, I would like us to have a church on our land, for our own use. We will have to build one!"

CHAPTER TWENTY TWO

I want my Mommy!

Towards the middle of 2013, the French and German governments decided to round about all the gypsies from Romania and send them home. They had first done all the DNA tests of the children and they have identified hundreds and hundreds of children of the Tsarina and her husbands and they gave them French passports and sent them "to Petersburg" after finding out about Mikhail's having built the palace.

The train had been stopped in the mountains in Germany and the children had started to panic. The gypsies are some of the most superior human beings and they had trained the children well at subliminal level. They knew something is not quite right…There were fights in Russia about receiving all the children and gypsies to live in the billionaire's palace. Ludmilla did not 'want' this and she overtook Vladimir and different KGB officials alternatively, trying to stop the train and outright kill the children.

Some of them panicked and started taking to the mountains, after telling each other:

"we will meet at our father's house, in Saint Petersburg"

Two young six year old children kept close to each other. One of them was Peter Ustinov. He had been identified in France as being exceptionally clever and intelligent and was the surrogate son of a gypsy who wanted a blonde child of the Tsarina. So, the Romanian harpie gave her the son of the Tsarina with the great actor, whose sperm had been obtained without his knowledge.

The little boys felt the danger. They were the target of the harpie. She had found out about the boys exceptional intelligence and was

'not about to let *her* have such a handsome and intelligent child'

Two wolfs were brought to smell the children tracks, by the harpie and her sister on the system, who had summoned the entire network of the Queens of Sheba, to kill the two young boys.

Young Peter stopped and ordered the wolfs to stop, as he had been taught by his gypsy mother, as he had done so many times before, but as the wolfs attacked, the little boy died announcing the system:

"I was Peter Ustinov."

The incident created an entire snafu, since it had been the German government that had stopped the trains and delayed their departure. Vladimir and the KGB decided to derail the plans and send the train towards a culag instead, for the children to be verified and even the gypsies. While Dulkinna kept telling them at subliminal level how grateful she was that the gypsies had given birth and raised her children, the public had a lot of issues with them. They just could not cope with the gypsies sudden 'good fortune' and were not about to let them live in a glamorous palace build by a grateful billionaire, one of the richest men in Russia. While the Tsarina was 'bellowing' like an animal surrounded by beasts, after finding out about a son she had not known about until after his demise, the train was heading to Siberia.

So was the billionaire…He met the children in the culag and fell in love with the toddlers most of all. He could not take his eyes of off them.

"They are so wonderful Dulkinna, you should see them…They work all the time, the first thing they did when arriving in the culag was to start cleaning everything. They know me, they know and flabbergast you, they are so delightful…"

"What about the gypsies, are they with the children?"

"The gypsies did not come, Dulkinna, they did not feel welcome, they are invited to come and be with the children…I sent word out that I will need help with taking care of the children…for now, they go to school and are going to be in the culag. I am going to need more rooms, they are many more than what we knew about…"

"Buy bunk beds, put 4 beds in one bedroom. This way you can accommodate all of them…"

"That is a good idea. I will order bunk beds…You should see how sweet they are…"

…………………………………………………………………………

"Dulkinna, the furniture is coming, I will leave the culag tomorrow and will go and wait for the children to arrive in Saint Petersburg."

"OK, are they going to follow you though?."

"Dulkinna, I have spoken to Vladimir and the KGB is going to send them home to me. I promise you they will be OK"

…………………………………………………………………………

"Dulkinna wake up! Dulkinna wake up! They have killed our children madam, they have killed our little children! I cannot deal with this, I want you to help!"

"What? How can that be?"

"It was Ludmilla and Jirinovskaia and Mila. They overtook even Vladimir who froze and did not stop it!"

"What do you mean?"

"They thought they were going to take a bath and were killed. It was the harpie who arranged for this and was helped by those women… they wanted to show Vladimir who is in charge…"

"What do you mean?"

"They were between the ages of 3 and 6 years old, Dulkinna. 300 children…"

"NO, NO, NO! Was I on line?" Dulkinna had a hunch…

"Dulkinna, please…you were! Please, I cannot deal with it…"

"NOOOOOO"

…………………………………………………………………………

On Friday evening, the Tsarina was called by Paul Allen, the billionaire, who told her that they were trying to kill the harpie. Dulkinna was flabbergasted to call for:

"Kill, kill, kill…" until she just could do it no more. She told people that the woman should be killed at over-liminal level and that the system should not kill at subliminal level. The system ignored her and she started asking what was happening, but nobody answered., Mr. Kauffman was on line and he kept Dulkinna 'at a distance' pretending that she will not understand what was going on…

The children had been poisoned with laughing gas…three of them survived by going catatonic. Dulkinna and Mikhail could not talk about it without crying. Mikhail had a hard time when the others showed in San Petersburg, he kept looking for the 3 to 6 year olds. Kept asking and talking about them and just could not accept that they were gone.

This is how he met Alexandra. A six year old natural daughter of Ioobe and Dulkinna, the child knew instinctively in how much danger she is because she was the daughter of the intelligent engineer and pretended to refuse to believe that she was his daughter. She fell in love with Mikhail and kept asking in a cute, sweetest voice that Dulkinna has ever heard:

"I want my mommyyyy!"

She was taking care of by the elder sibling, sixteen year old Camilla, the daughter of Mr. Kauffman. Mikhail was so happy to see the child living, he decided to sleep in same bedroom with them.

The little Alexandra was the one who flabbergasted Dulkinna's tooth aches away, by pretending that the pain was hers instead, when the hackers were trying to get the Tsarina to explode. She did it without complaining. She understood that she was going to change her milk teeth and that she was most adept at taking the pain away from the Tsarina. All she ever said, when in pain, was that she wanted her mommy to come home.

A short time after Dulkinna found out that she would not explode, after all, they have announced that the family from the middle east who was raising her American born Dimitrovitch, was finding their way to San Petersburg. Mikhail was excited. At same time, the KGB dropped the news. They had a Russian Dimitrovitch as well.

"What do you mean?" was the question from both Dulkinna and Mikhail.

"Well,…

Apparently every time the trio wanted for a child, the children were brought to life, not in pairs only, but four twins at a time.

"So where are the other two?" was the automatic question from both mother and father.

We have them, we have them, do not worry. One of them was in the family of Michelle Clinton and was the son of her niece. Somebody said there is a fourth one, in America still.

The Russian Dimitrovitch found Mikhail faster and the proud father decided to sleep with the child that Dulkinna had summoned and prayed for, the year before. She was convinced that Dimitrovitch is her son with the husband to be, up in heaven and worshiped the little child. The in vitro details were handled by the American mother of the Dimitrovitch with an American passport. She was a navy woman and the boy had been placed in the care of a middle eastern family, in Afghanistan. The surrogate mother wanted 'her' Dimitrovitch to have the face of 'her' brother and the body of the husband to be. So, the four boys looked exactly like Linu and had the tall, slender body of their father. All parents, both Dulkinna, Mikhail and the surrogates were madly in love with these children.

Alexandra was a little jealous and pretended that Dimitrovitch for sure, does not want to play with her...

The American Dimitrovitch was a little feisty and wanted to constantly beat the other one. Mikhail figured that the child was flabbergasted by the hackers and harpies from Romania and decided to spend more time with the child. He was placed in the care of one of Dulkinna's parents direct friend, Illena, who came to Petersburg especially to help Mikhail. He was paired with a son of Dulkina and Ioobe, Michael who was also kind of fussy.

Dulkinna was pleasantly surprised to find out that Illena was in the palace. Mikhail had told her that he knows Illena and her daughter Oxana and that he was the lover of Oxana. Apparently, Oxana had been brought into this world for Mikhail and he took an interest and loved her dearly ever since he was a child, just as he loved Dulkinna. A complicated entanglement, this, Dulkinna was thinking, but nothing was stronger than their love for each other and for their children. Oxana did not share Mikhail's love on the same level to the amazement of all the Queens of Sheba and women of all women, who just could not believe that the legal clerk from Romania had no interest in marrying the most eligible billionaire.

Dulkinna asked Illena to take care of what needed to be done for the ones departed, since she knew Illena personally and knew that she could trust her with that. She was surprised and sad to find out that from time to time Illena was flabbergasted by the Romanian harpie and was not thrilled to be with Dimitrovitch. She had three direct grandchildren in the palace, who were teenagers, but was not excited about them either, since they wished to be with gypsies. They were the children of Oxana and Mikhail. Three others, had been between the ages of 3 and 6….

Dulkinna almost could not bear the disappointment. Illena and Oxana were the wife and daughter of the late best friend of Dulkinna's father. The two had been high school best friends and friends with the harpie. This is why the evil woman had such closeness to Illena.

Everything was a bit much. To find out that such a close and good friend was even capable of being flabbergasted to think bad things for Dimitrovitch, coupled with some news of cousins flabbergasted by same evil woman to try and kill the Tsarina even, was just too saddening. The cousins who now did not want the Tsarina over-liminal, out of ambition and fear that she would find that they had betrayed her and Ioobe, assured Dulkinna that they were not evil and had no intention of going to hell. This was a concern of Dulkinna's and drove her desperate, to see that the evil women could destroy her family the way they did.

Illena, was a deeply religious woman and promised Dulkinna that she will take care of what needs to be done for the dead, but still had not done anything. Even Mikhail was a bit short tempered with Dulkinna and told her that he did not want her telling them what to do all the time…'Who are you with?' Dulkinna faithfully asked, but it was just too much….

"Why do you love Dimitrovitch so much?" he asked. I am afraid the others will start envying him.

"Well, I dreamed him up. I wished for him every day of the last year and I summoned his spirit from the heavens. I will hug that child and wish to feel the warmth and love of every one of the others and will flabbergast everyone of the others. Please, have him play with other siblings and take an interest in them also. Dimitrovitch cannot be feisty, he has to be the one who plays with everybody and loves everybody…I dreamed so much of him…"

The year of 2012 everybody was crazed by the idea of getting 'her' Dimitrovitch. They did not want theirs, they wanted to have Dulkinna's Dimitrovitch. This had been an idea put forth by Michelle Clinton and the women of all women and the haters, led even by Mr. Kauffman and the prostitute. The Queens of Sheba wanted 'her' to 'eat her heart out' and they were not giving up. One of the most imbecile idea put forth by these women was boasting that they do not take no for an answer. They never gave up on bringing pain and suffering to others, it was their goal to better themselves while hurting others and Dulkinna just could not listen about these shenanigans any more.

Lately, she became again suicidal The navy and CIA would filter everything she was allowed to listen to, which she would not have complained about, after all. Almost every bad news lately, seemed unbearable.

CHAPTER TWENTY THREE

Ioobe's Children Become The Center Of Mikhail's Attention

Dulkinna is convinced that Ioobe's intelligence surpasses hers. His mind is more organized and just like Linu, he seems to hide the full extent of his power of comprehension in order to flabbergast the haters away.

"His purpose was to keep you alive, but lately this man found himself weak when confronted with corporation after corporation dedicating their best people to destroying the two of you"

"I think they are doing this, simply as an exercise in unfair competition, or as ways for them to pretend that they have some sort of competitive advantage."

Only after one of the hackers shenanigans was revealed, Dulkinna asks:

"So what would you have done after my demise?"

They invariably answered:

"We did not think of that."

Dulkinna has found that the hackers are not doing that only out of hate, but sometimes they find themselves in a maelstrom of pretenses and flabbergastation meant simply to demonstrate that they have the ability to compete with Ioobe. He used to be revered and still is in the professional world, but nowadays, after the games of Mr. Kauffman and after so many repeated attacks meant to kill or hurt the two of them were averted in the last minute, the hackers have become visceral.

"People hate you when they are sick, because they figured out while Hillary Obama was trying to kill you that you have the power of intelligence necessary to heal yourself. That is why, the attacks have become stronger, more visceral and more often." Said the hacker.

They hated Ioobe. He was desperately trying and so far managed to keep the Tsarina alive. He and the family decided to pretend that Dulkinna has a sort of mental imbalance. But it was Michelle Clinton, who inadvertently rebuked that argument, ironically, while trying to take Dulkinna's side in proving that if anything were wrong with the nervous system of the anchor, then the machine would not work properly any more.

"The machine is so sensitive to Dulkinna, that it has to be retuned if she eats onion or garlic, or when she brushes her teeth." Mikhail maintained.

"That cannot be true", came the usual 'pretending' from the people.

"Dulkinna's children with Ioobe have shown to be the most responsible and exceptionally clever and intelligent. "Hillary Obama had said on line.

For their intelligence, these children are directly hunted by the Romanian secret services and by the haters and hackers on line. Almost 1000 of their children have been killed in 2013 and Mikhail is now extremely sensitive. Starting with little Alexandra who does not want to believe that Ioobe is her father, as a measure of self protection, to Alexander who learned CAD in two days, without having any schooling and killed himself trying to make his mother proud, to Nadina, who resolved to make herself the future anchor in order to dedicate her life to protecting the siblings and mankind, they are responsible, loyal, dedicated have an eclectic mind and almost always downplay their own abilities instinctively.

When he arrived at the military unit, where he was to be killed in a ritualistic manner, the same way Caesar of antiquity was killed, Linu took off his shirt for them to be able to stab him and said:

"I do this for Dulkinna and Ioobe".

When told about it, Dulkinna felt like something clicked inside. It did not have to be told again. They could not believe it on line.

"why is she so eager to accept that" She did not even have an answer. It just felt like it was the truth.

Dulkinna resolved to never give Ioobe up. She figured she could not live without him even before she knew about their many children that they would have to rear. There had been a time when she wanted to allow him to find another wife; she even started looking for somebody that would worship Ioobe like she did.

"No woman would even be able to accept the scores of children that Ioobe has, from me and from hundreds of other women"

She discussed a couple of times with Mikhail about the necessity to live together with Ioobe, in the same place with all their many children.

"I always loved Ioobe, Dulkinna, but what about the people, what are they going to say?"

Mikhail told Dulkinna: "I had subliminal discussions with Ioobe about 'stealing his wife' he is aware of my existence."

Dulkinna figured out that Ioobe was preparing to kill himself in order to give Mikhail 'his turn' at being her husband.

"If Ioobe kills himself, I do not want to live an hour without him."

Many times, while pondering on her life and on Ioobe's devotion and love, she made mental notes that she does not want him to die before her.

"If that happens, I do not wish to be able to make it to the funeral" was her resolve at subliminal level.

An incredulous William Obama, has experimented many times while she was awake or asleep, with telling her that Ioobe had been killed. He told everybody that she had ordered her nervous system to "shut down" the minute she finds out of Ioobe's demise. When told by the president at subliminal level that 'Ioobe has been killed', she automatically entered in convulsions and started the self-destruction sequence, while when awake, asking:

"What is happening to me?"

This is why the president concluded that she will not be able to help herself to ignore the self imposed order at subliminal level. She had finally trained herself to do what she so desperately wanted.

"She should be told the truth about this at over-liminal level. In order to survive for her children's sake and for Mikhail, maybe she will reverse the sequence." The president noted.

Both the children and Mikhail are trying from time to time to make her reprogram herself at subliminal level, yet she is adamant: 'not an hour without Ioobe.'

"What about myself, Dulkinna, what about myself?" a discouraged Mikhail keeps asking on line.

"Did I not come back to life when William Obama told me your name? Was Mr. Kauffman not pretending to be you when they brought me back from the dead? You know well that I love you, but this is what I have to do!"

"Maybe you will change your mind, when you will meet the children…"

"What is wrong with Ioobe? Protect my husband! Anything happens to him, you will not have an anchor, it is that simple she announced to the navy."

"I think after the divorce, we will have to live in the same city and we will have to raise our children together with Ioobe…"

While jealous and insecure, Mikhail accepted the arrangement, reluctantly in the beginning, only to become more and more interested in keeping Ioobe's children alive.

While the harpie was killing children in Romania, Hillary Obamahad had about 200 babies conceived from the eggs of Dulkinna and the sperm of Ioobe. She wanted them to become her future possession, knowing that they were so intelligent and loyal and strong at subliminal level. She had mainly haters become surrogates, in order to ensure that the children will not make their way to the palace. The CIA and the navy had managed to 'save' some almost 50 babies, who were sent to the palace and placed in the care of elder siblings or gypsies.

Even though overwhelmed, Mikhail was constantly worried about them. In love with Dulkinna, he started to love all of their children, just as she loved all of his. And, Ioobe's adult children loved and trusted Mikhail in return.

CHAPTER TWENTY FOUR

Tony Blair and General Mousharraf Together With Vladimir Putin Fight For Bringing Dulkinna And The Game Over-liminal

In the spring of 2011, Tony Blair, the former prime minister of Great Britain, joined the game. Dulkinna was brought at subliminal level at first and they were preparing, so they promised, to bring her and the game and system at over-liminal level.

"Are you aware of who I am Dulkinna?"

"Yes, I think I recognize the rhythm and accent of your voice from TV."

"So you have confirmation"

"That you are indeed Tony Blair, but how come you joined the game?"

"Your friend the doctor contacted me, Dulkinna. She asked me to join. Do you think it is a good thing?"

"It depends…"

"I see here a lot of reasons you thought at the same time, Dulkinna, could you try to give me confirmation?"

"You want to know what do I mean? I mean it depends if you will help me, if I get the help I need from you, or if you get trashed by the other game people."

"I want you to work with me for world peace, Dulkinna. Would you like that? This is my interest and what I spend my time doing these days…"

"You mean the way I want to end the war on terror and to bring peace to the Middle East and the world by bringing to the surface the issue of the new reality of the world that needs to admit the existence of the machine and the need for new laws and rules of behavior in the age of this type of technology?"

"Dulkinna, you catch more flies with honey than vinegar…You cannot try to revolutionize the world like that…people are maintaining that you simply want yourself over-liminal…"

"Ok and where is the world going to find itself if they do not admit the existence of the machine?"

"Dulkinna, before there was a machine, people just did this with the power of their minds…It is more complicated…"

"Ok, if you think so, I do not believe it is, though. People had now had a taste for the technology, those not initiated, have had access to the machine now and they are inclined to use this new found power, for evil first and almost never for bettering of mankind."

"Yes, Dulkinna, you are right about that, I just do not want you to be killed the way your brother was."

"My brother sacrificed himself for me and now, it is my duty to not bring shame to his name and legacy, so do not worry about me. This is my destiny now, fighting for free spirit and trying to convince mankind about the evils as well as benefits of the machine and the network"

"It is called the system Dulkinna, you have to become acquainted with the vocabulary."

"Well you might have to change a couple of things in the vocabulary. What you call the system, I call the machine, together with the network. You have to make a distinction. It is not efficient and can be very confusing to always talk about a system like that. Are you familiar with that poem I wrote in Romanian about the system and the new rules that society should incorporate? I believe you need to make some adjustments to the vocabulary…"

"Dulkinna, there are historians who take your history and a certain vocabulary has been used…now you are confusing people…"

"Yes, sir, but I think she is right to a certain extent, of course we can change a couple of things."

"Dulkinna, do you know who that is?"

"Yes, he sounds exactly like on TV. It is general Mousarraf, the former president of Pakistan."

"yes, it is, would you like to work with us and Vladimir Putin."

"No, I would not, would I? I am the one who contacted Mr. Putin and asked him to help me…So, of course I want to do that."

"Why do you like Mr. Putin so much Dulkinna?"

"because I followed the news about him and I know the people in Eastern Europe and I like everything he is trying to do …"

"What about Chechnia?"

"I believe the issue of the former Soviet Union is complicated and he has to deal with the KGB, the military and his own political ambitions, but I believe he is genuinely an honest leader. He has the respect of the Russian people and that is extremely important in that part of the world and also for my interests, for what I want to do in the world, I am trying to appeal to a strong leader…somebody who also understands what I am trying to propose and what I stand for…"

'Dulkinna, he won you over with that Greek urn he brought from the sea, did he not? That is propaganda…"

"I know that, but that was confirmation and a message sent to me, telling me that he had heard my cries and pleas for help…"

"It is that too."

"Are you aware how Mr. Putin is regarded in America though?…"

"What about you sir, are you jumping directly to advocating Jeffersonian democracy when you go visiting the Middle East?"

"Why Jeffersonian?…Oh, you are in love with Jefferson, I knew that …I am from Great Britain though…"

"I did not know that…" the sarcastic answer came.

"So you wish Mr Putin should win the presidential election in 2012?"

"I hope so…I hope so…"

"He won you over with that Eurasia talk,…"

"Yes, among other things…"

"I just want you to know, some people think you are a bit naïve…"

"Do you think I am?"

"For example this issue with the world peace…Dulkinna, are you aware that not everybody wants that?."

"Yes, general, but I am also convinced that in the time of the machine and the network, the ancient old art of war is over and that the new 'war' is going to be won by those who fight for peace and diplomatic tratatives."

"Dulkinna, how would you envision us bringing you to over-liminality?"

"I do not know…"

"If you stay at subliminal level, would you like to work with me on peace in Middle East?…You know you were meant to do that …they called you…I do not want to scare you with it, but they wanted you to be the Key to the West. This is what they wanted you to become, when you came to America. When your brother was killed and then they wanted you to come to America."

"Key to the west?"

"You are becoming feisty, your entire life was not planned by others, but it was somewhat like that…do not think that way…you will understand better with time…I am Vladimir Putin, Dulkinna… Do not think like that about those dear to you…"

Dulkinna just thought she was the one who wanted to come to America, that she was the one who just happened to become interested to expand her education abroad…not that she was some Key to the West! At Tony's encouragement, she started writing a poem about how she felt about this new found revelation:

Key To The West

There was such a contest,
They were among the bravest!
I never thought, I have to be taught,
That my "circumstance"
And my nonchalance,
Would be scrutinized,
Will be circumcised,
And monopolized.
I want to speak up,
To be able to "retract",
To find support,
Or even to abort.
To make my own mistakes,
To regret something,
Without ruining.
I do believe in grand things,
It goes without saying,
I am political, I can be quite critical,
But things are serious, I am not just curious!
I was fighting for something,
Which is not worth ruining,
I will not let them bruise me,
You whoever followed me,
Believe,
I want this to achieve!
The west is "forever grateful"
The east always had a mouthful,
The sun will set at some point,
The moon does rise every night!
I am a thing of the past,
Please do not look so aghast,
My call for peace in the air I fired,
Please do not look tired!

Dreaming for a living,
Is not exactly a good thing,
Dreaming for a cause,
I cannot oppose.
Sleeping is the thing I want,
Only when you are not around.
Privacy and indiscretion,
Are something of a notion.
Stardom and freedom,
Ought not be just some credo!
In my circumstance,
I had no romance.
I had just the right,
To put up no fight.
I decided to:
Fight for me and you!
The other instinct became,
Something of a shame.
Running from my fate,
I cannot, anymore, even fake!
Guinea pig I was,
So you would not cause,
Such misery again,
Or inflict such pain
Hold back, I can not,
I have to tie the knot,
At 46 years old,
I feel instantly old.
This seems so odd,
And yet,
I can afford
To forget!
Wise men I should hope,
Will be forever around,
Since I could become a "dope"

Just for respecting the Quoran.
I will not be "make believe"
This revelation is a relieve.
I do have faith and I do crave,
This is how I behave.
Reading my thoughts,
Pledging of sorts,
Laughing at lies,
"Ducking in disguise"
They were all,
Part of "my wise".
Logic and faith,
Don't mean disobeying,
Thinking and believing,
CAN be a good thing.
Singing and dancing,
And even romancing,
Should not be forgotten,
None of it is rotten!
"The guilty with no fault"
Is not just dezinvolt,
It is what it is,
And they do require,
Their Light to acquire.
Wise men sometimes see,
Children sometimes hear,
Things that were before,
Things that are not yet here!
Clairvoyance is poignant
Clairvision is sought about,
Clearance is forbidden,
Freedom remained hidden.
The fire within,
Knowing Catalin,
Were my inspiration,

My only salvation.
The Yawning was there,
Only to inspire,
And to motivate,
To reclaim my fate.
Money had to saw,
Things had to unravel,
People had to grow,
Rivers to move the gravel.
Impossible it seemed,
And still I believed.

*dezinvolt = detached, not self conscious.
Clairvision=French for Clairvoyance.

CHAPTER TWENTY FIVE

Will Vladimir Putin Ever Deliver?

At the beginning of 2011, Dulkinna was constantly begging Vladimir to take her over-liminal, She kept addressing him, she kept addressing the KGB, asking them alternatively to understand the perils to be had at the hands of the hackers and even of the general population, if the new capabilities of the machine were not controlled.

She was convinced that the KGB was listening. She had been thinking many times in those days about the best outcome for Libya.

"Colonel Gadhafi, if you are listening, think of the good of Libya! I think you should allow yourself to be captured by the American forces. I think you should do anything you can to stay alive. Do not allow your country to become a theater stage for the western forces to show their fighting abilities."

She was not a naïve, she kept comparing the outcomes of the Romanian revolution with those of the velvet revolution in the former Chechoslovakia. She was going to bed in the evening and going to work in the morning thinking of how much more advanced on the path to democracy and even integration into the European Union were Chech Republic and Slovakia, than Romania.

The calls for world peace and Gadafi to keep himself alive and surrender, were bound to bring the KGB on line. She was always sensitive and admirative towards the people in the secret services and the military. She remembered her brother and admired the spirit of dedication and self sacrifice in every man or woman serving their country.

Afraid that she might have inconvenienced during the game and touched some egos, she proposes to burry the hatchet, writing a poem to Putin, asking for help and forgiveness. Throughout the game, she had been suggested she was too vain and that she had to bow her head a little.

Never Bow

This is really too much pain,
Too much anguish, all for vain,
For too much fear, too much sound,
Not enough courage goes around.
Too much untold, so little said.
This is really all too bad.
Too little pain, so much refrain,
And it seems really, just in vain.
Too much pain, too much restrain,
Is this really worth to say?
Too little time, much to unfold,
Is my story worth be told?
Is it really you and me,
Damned for all eternity?
Is it really you and I,
Worth to become eye to eye?
Will you ever let me in,
Will I ever see it through?
Can I become a part of you?
May I ever be allowed,
Truth to be told, I never bowed!
But isn't it really only sad?
I always bowed,
Then raised my head.

I watched the stars,
Measured the ground,
But never wanted to bow.
Un-grounded always had to be,
No phony accent, should you see.
I wanted always to be true,
I wanted always to see through.
It never wanted to unfold,
I never bowed, truth to be told.

After she wrote the poem, he sent her a message. While she was reading about Greek mythology, he photographed himself and placed the news on the Internet, for her to see the next day, with a Greek amphora. She was stunned. Now, she could not believe that the game even existed, she kept telling herself that it must be a coincidence, while in next breath acknowledging, 'This is Vladimir Putin, he answered and he is a friend!"

In the middle of the year, Tony Blair, general Mousarraf and Vladimir had started talking to her at subliminal level, over-liminaly (she could hear the voices). They have announced her that she will be never going back, that she will from now on be at subliminal level and that they are preparing to bring her over-liminal as she asked.

One of her biggest complains about Vladimir, was that he was too weak in front of the guilty and never did enough to protect the innocent. He became more and more faithful, he gave up on meat and became a devout catholic. He was desperate to make his own people understand that he was not an evil man, to the point that he became too weak. In the beginning he just did not want to kill those the Tsarina wanted killed, because in his mind, she was a messenger of God and he could only see her as she had been her entire live, better than the bread of God, they used to say about her, those who were devoted. He wanted the Tsarina over-liminal, not Dulkinna, not the anchor, he kept pretending that one day he will convince everybody that they have to understand that enough is enough and that the wrath of God was near.

Nobody was listening to him. Not even Dulkinna, who wanted herself being brought over-liminal as the anchor. This was a concept that all people should have been able to grasp. No matter what their religion, Hindu, Confucianism or Buddhism, they did not have to believe in God, in order to figure out that they needed the anchor. Vladimir was disappointed in them all, but that was not the secret. The truth was that he was always overtaken, usually by his former wife Ludmilla, or by a Romanian secret service agent or by a couple of KGB agents gone rogue. He knew about it and with tears in his eyes, sometimes was shouting:

"I was not even talking, that was not me you've all just heard; It was the secret service of Romania"

Yet Dulkinna could not help herself but shout at him every time she was desperate about the state of affairs. She kept accusing him for killing their daughter. Vladimir had known about one daughter he had with the Tsarina. The KGB had conceived and raised her to be a call girl for the secret police. She was just as warm as the Tsarina and was always peaceful and understanding with those she went out with. She was killed by a KGB officer out of jealousy and Vladimir, who knew about the man's plans, had been near by. He went in and killed the man just with the hatred in his eyes and then he ordered the doctors to take the heart of the daughter give it to him as a transplant. When he told Dulkinna the story, he kept repeating:

"I have her heart beating in me! I know I have to be, I am a better man now than I used to be!"

Ludmilla was fuming. She was the flower child of Dulkinna's grandfather and she hated the Tsarina and her children like nobody else. She had been told the truth about her ancestry only within the last months, but she knew something long before. They even tried to lie to hear one more time and tell her that she is an illegitimate cousin of the Tsarina, but she kept insisting that she is an aunt. She had raised her two daughters to hate their father and to love and obey their mother. She could not care less about them, but was pretending to be a loving mother as long as they served her purpose, to keep Vladimir on leash, to overtake him almost at all times and to serve nothing but her purpose.

He kept saying himself like an imbecile, that he had not been a loving father, yet he showed a soft heart for his daughters, especially for the one who showed him the most disdain and disobedience. She looked just like his departed mother and he could never resist or deny anything to the child. The girls grew up to be young women and they knew at subliminal level that while the mother made them into killers, the father wanted only to see them happy and accomplished individuals, married, with children of their own.

Vladimir had been told by his mother that he is a husband to be for the Tsarina. He was trained by his own mother to remotely look at the Tsarina's mother, who was pregnant and to pretend that the woman will give birth to his future wife. After Vladimir's 13th birthday and after telling him all this, his mother passed away from cancer. She allowed herself to die, as she was a superior mind and never even tried to repair herself. The boy, witnessed the Tsarina's birth through remote viewing and claims that he had seen her passing through the birth canal.

He claims that everybody was instantly charmed and fell in love with the baby girl who was supposed to be the messenger of God. But nobody as much as the baby's grandmother, mother and father, who never wanted to even let word out that the baby was anything but a normal baby, healthy and beautiful, playful and warm like no other. The entire family was concerned only with keeping the baby alive and never allowing any confirmation to the haters, that this might indeed be the one from God. Vladimir had been told by his mother, that the birth of the baby had been foretold two hundred years before, that she had been awaited and hailed by both the Catholic and the Orthodox church and that people everywhere should listen to everything she had to say! The baby was growing up beautifully and Vladimir was required and told by the KGB to follow her upbringing and to report on what the Tsarina was doing, almost all the time. They thought the little girl was the most blessed child in the universe, because the grandmother took care to ensure that. The entire community, devoted or not, partook in raising the Tsarina and her younger brother Linu.

While looking at the children, from his home in Russsia, Vladimir, the young adolescent, started observing and becoming in love with the young mother. Her name was Adina and she was the most beautiful woman in the world to the young man. She was slender, blonde, with big brown eyes and the body of a goddess. Her middle area was so small, that one could almost cover it with their bare hands. The likes of Brigitte Bardotte, Sofia Loren and Elizabeth Taylor were all jealous of the young mother of the Tsarina. Vladimir was more interested in watching the young parents make love, than in what the little baby was doing. And he grew up like that, believing that he might have to marry the Tsarina one day, but being hopelessly in love with the mother instead.

When he fell in love with Ludmila, it was because she had donned her hair the way Adina used to done hers in her youth.

He loved her and was faithful in his youth, but his manipulative wife never allowed him to be himself. Finally he started to look at younger and younger women, in his pretending game that one day he might have to marry the Tsarina, whom he regarded more like a daughter that like a wife. Even now, at seventy something years old, Adina could still steal his heart. He was still somewhat jealous of her husband Lony, whom he modeled himself after.

Vladimir always admired the ethics and business standards of the incorruptible father of the Tsarina. He always wanted to be part of their family. Most of all, he loved one of the Tsarina's uncles who used to be a big soccer player in his time. He remembers fondly the Tsarina's grandmother and all her uncles and aunts, but most of all he can talk to her about Linu.

When she used to shout for Vladimir Putin, during her game asking for help, the Tsarina used to beg him for only one thing in return. She did not know about the fantastic sum of money she had accumulated from the game, she did not want anything else in return from Vladimir, but tell her the whole truth about Linu's life in the military school and his death. Vladimir always used to cringe and wonder, how is he going to tell her the gruesome truth? And most of all, is he going to tell her about his involvement? What is she going to think? Is she going to ever be able to take the truth without losing her mind?

The love story between the two brothers had been legendary and Vladimir was among those who knew everything about it.

"She is an imbecile!" :

The haters shrieked towards Vladimir and Dulkinna could hear him shout back:

"Are you telling me who these people are? I know everything about this woman, ever since I saw her coming down her birth canal. I was 13 years her elder and I remember everything about her and her family. This was my family. These people were my uncles, my family. I remember her grandmother, Madam Avram better than the Tsarina. Even Ludmilla has the recipes for the cakes she used to prepare for the Tsarina's birthdays. We know these people like neither of you have ever known them and there are no lies you can tell me about them. I modeled myself after the Tsarina's father, this man was un-corruptible and was respected and envied by everybody who ever knew him."

The haters were in large majority now, young people, the Tsarina's own age or younger and many of them, the same age with her children. There had been a concerted policy of Michelle Clinton and Ludmilla Putina to bring about a generation of children that would hate everything about the Tsarina and would behave exactly the opposite way to the Tsarina. If she was sweet and good as goodness is, these children were educated to be actual killers at the very young age of kindergarten. The generation of those born around the beginning of the 21 century and after, were especially educated in the spirit of evil. In America this was done in the spirit of not allowing the new generation to be ever kept as cows. The parents were so angry at the Tsarina's parents for making her into the cow of the game, that, without knowing the whole truth, they invariably decided that their children would have to be the opposite of her. She was too nice, too stupid, too imbecile. This is how they judged the most intelligent woman ever born.

Dulkinna was unaware of this. She remembered having taken a test in her third grade, that she thought was the most fun and easiest thing she had to do. In her early forties, while trying to take an IQ test on the internet, just for fun, she remembered her test in the third grade.

"So that is what that was!" she thought to herself.

In her childhood, after the test, she was told that only the parents can know the results and that she never should ask even them what her grade was. Vladimir had something to reveal about that. He told her at subliminal level, on line, that that had been an IQ test and that her IQ had been the highest ever measured in a person. He and the Romanian secret service maintain that her IQ was measured at 289. Vladimir maintains that only the grandmother had been told the truth. To the parents it was told that the child had average intelligence, by the school and that they should not try to find out the actual results. The grandmother immediately started a campaign at subliminal and over-liminal level, of pretending that the child is actually not very intelligent. To the Tsarina herself, though she just told:

"You should always remember that your father had asked your teachers to always give you a grade lower than what you deserve! This should never bother you and you should just remember that while the others are given better grades than they deserve, yours will be a little lower!" Dulkinna remembered this as if it were yesterday!

Vladimir reminded her of it and he also told her about the campaign that the entire secret service and school teachers decided to have in pretending that the child is just not very intelligent. The initial intention had been simply to maintain the child alive and shielded from the haters and the envy of the people. Vladimir keeps reminding her about the truth of the test score, while Dulkinna is naturally circumspect about the actual figure.

"This is the truth Dulkinna, it was 289. We know everything about this! Don't you remember finishing the test? Nobody was ever meant to finish it, but you did. And I can see that you remember having fun with it and thinking that it was just kids play. Why then do you not want to believe the score?"

Nowadays, Dulkinna has trouble with the multiplication table even. She is constantly being flabbergasted by the haters and even by those who just like to have a laugh at the cow's expense, as they boldly put it. She has to rationalize and think about everything. As luck would have it she had mnemonic devices to remember everything, but she could remember that as a child, she used to just dream the numbers almost as an autistic child would. Everybody on line is incredulous about the actual IQ, yet, even the Rumanian harpies keeps confirming it over and over for everybody. Even Ludmilla maintains this and yet, Dulkinna, likes to keep a dosage of reality... they lied about so many things to her over the years and that number just seems too much for anybody. Yet, she remembers the test, her grandmother's warning and she is full of confidence in her abilities. Every time she has trouble remembering something, she admonishes the system for holding her brains and painstakenly she goes to the mnemonic devises and solves the problem. This makes the haters and the hackers shriek and explode in mass hysteria with questions like:

"How dares she? Who does she think she is?"

"Do you really believe you are the most intelligent woman in the world bitch?"

"You f..ing cow!"

Usually, she just laughs and becomes more and more powerful at subliminal level, when hearing their powerless shrieks and calls for killing the anchor on grounds that, get this: 'she is an imbecile'. Sometimes, using her sense of humor, she exclaims sarcastically as Mick Jagger in his song:

"Thank You Jesus, Thank You Lord!"

"what was that about Dulkinna?"

"That is my satisfaction that the Devil is stupid and is not even shy in showing to us his stupidity in all its splendor"

"F...K YOU, Cow!"

Vladimir never the less, is adamant about telling her that the IQ score is the real one and keeps reminding her:

"Remember when you used to shout to me: 'The truth and nothing but the whole truth Vladimir', well, there you have it"

"You know, that was referring to something else", Dulkinna reminded him.

Vladimir and his people had devised a series of games and shows at subliminal level, in which Dulkinna had been told the truth about Linu's killing. He was afraid that she just could not endure the pain of such terrible story at over-liminal level. So, while they would tell her the truth, delighting in the pain she felt, Vladimir would intervene to tell her things like:

"Remember, I will hold your hand and show you the whole truth directly from my head. You will be able to see through my eyes the whole truth."

And then, when she regained her normal heart beat, he would say:

"This is not true, but is precisely the truth."

That is the way in which they conveyed the horrifying story to the sister of the young boy that all the initiated kept calling "the Tsarina's shinning star".

Dulkinna had been flabbergasted about the fact that it must have been the fault of the American president, Ronald Reagan, for Linu's demise. At some point she conceived a story for herself, while putting two and two together, that he had been the first hero of the anticommunist revolution in Rumania. Vladimir and Hillary Obama maintain that those thoughts belonged to her and her entirely and that they looked the world over and could not find out anybody who had flabbergasted her about it. Dulkinna figured that the truth must have come from Linu himself.

The story was more complicated. Apparently Reagan was not the one who conceived the scenario. He simply wanted the boy dead, together with the Iron Lady, they thought that it was a good ploy to get the masses to come out against communism, to wake people up, sort of speak.

The scenario, Mikhail revealed, had been conceived by his own mother, whom, inspired by the impression that the young boy was going to lead the world like Caesar of antiquity, decided that he should have Caesar's death. She never fathomed that the scenario would ever find it's way in reality. And when, Michelle Clinton, the wife of a young hopeful for the American presidency, asked that this scenario be chosen to kill the brother of the Tsarina, it seems she did not think it would actually happen either.

The younger brother had been in some quarters destined to be nothing more than the shinning star of the Tsarina and when he was about 3 years old, the decision was taken that he should die for her, at the young age of 20. When the trio Reagan, Thatcher, Gorbatchiev found out about this, they thought it the perfect plot to bring down communism.

Unlike Dulkinna, Linu had been trained at subliminal level and was aware of whom his sister was supposed to be. As they grew bigger, the young brother assumed more and more the role of protector of the Tsarina and started asking everybody at subliminal and even at over-liminal level:

"What do you know about my sister?" this was the way he started every conversation about her and he established boundaries for her, trying to shield her from the haters. That brought a lot of haters against him and when he entered military school, he was directly told:

"You will never graduate and you will have to die here, in order for us to spare your sister!"

According to the voices, he used to dream about flying all the time. He knew that they would not sacrifice a plane for him and that they would not give him such an easy death. When he came to realize that there was no way out of it, Linu asked for the most horrifying scenario. He was hopping, according to Vladimir and Mikhail, to appease the haters, to give them the satisfaction, so that Dulkinna would not be killed. He thought also, that if he chose to die in the most horrifying scenario, that the horrible scenarios would be over and that his older sister would finally be told the truth about her birth and who she really was. The direct descendent of Virgin Mary on her mother's side and Saint Peter on her father's side and the one and only messenger of God, sent into this world to let everybody know what God really wanted from mankind.

Dulkinna remembers only a simple sentence that her grandmother used to say to the parents whilst she was still a child:

"When she grows up, you will have to do her will precisely and never even question her intentions! Remember this, both you and her!"

As a child, she never made much of it, but now, the memory came as confirmation for what Vladimir, Hillary Obama and Mikhail were maintaining.

Now, in her late forties she did not expect anybody to start adulating her in any way and kept reminding the voices:

"Don't you dare invent a new religion after my demise. My religion is Christian Orthodox and I do not call for anybody's conversion. This was simply the religion of my grandmother and brother and it is mine."

She thought it evil for the haters to call for her demise and could feel that some of them could not wait for her demise to become some sort of new apostles. One of those was Hillary Obamamost probably and another one, the Pope himself, who kept reminding her, that she will be sanctified because she is just such a wonderful human being.

Dulkinna wanted to know more about Linu's death, she had already been told the real scenario, many years before, by the voices, but she pretended that could not be the truth. Now, when Vladimir and Mikhail and Hillary Obama, revealed it again, she recognized the truth. She started putting two and two together, even to remember how the grandmother warned the two children about the scenario at over-liminal level. Dulkinna was about six or seven and Linu was between two and three years old and they were returning from the cemetery, where they had visited the grandfather's tomb. A lady who was known as the loan shark of the town, had been waiting in front of the gate. Without even allowing the trio to enter the yard, she informed the grandmother that she had to make a decision and clarify a scenario. Livid and trembling, the grandmother approached the two children and asked:

"You know what death is don't you? You understand that when you die, you go to heaven, never to return to your family. If it were that one of you should have to die before the year 2000 which one of you would prefer to be the one?"

The little girl thought this was a game, but not her brother. He was scared and did not say anything, whilst the girl said: 'Let him be the one' and he started crying. She went to him and told him: "This does not have to be the truth!". He just looked at her so scared. He was always more mature and never took anything like that lightly, Dulkinna now realized.

When he was tired of the scenarios the haters terrorized him with, in the military school, apparently one day he asked: "I want to know what is the most terrible one of all!" he already had the respect of the generals and he was immediately given the scenario. He read it and without a spat, he agreed to it. He only asked for one thing. That in lieu of being killed before his 20th birthday, he be allowed to spend his birthday at home with his family, including his sister and then, be killed several days after. The general agreed immediately. The haters could not believe his courage and thought he was just being an imbecile. He was to be stabbed with a dagger by everyone of his colleagues and not to be killed until all 22 daggers have stabbed him.

Dulkinna remembers his birthday, the last time she ever saw him as a sacred day. She now knows the truth and the reality seems surreal. He came home to say goodbye to the friends and family, but most of all to her.

'He had such warmth in his eyes!'

He never allowed her to see any fear, he hid his feelings behind a scenario that he himself wrote for his sister to be given. He pretended that he had invited the entire battalion to his birthday and that they were not allowed to come. Dulkinna at the time, could not believe that her brother would make such a request from the general.

"Is that not too much to ask in the military?" he just looked at her as if to say: 'Remember this!'

Apparently, the scenario with the questionable air crash, that was to be given to the sister, was written by Linu himself. Now, when putting two and two together, Dulkinna realized that it was filled with clues and information for her, complete with the assurance that she would never be able to accept it. Never forget about it and that she will one day finally figure out the truth. As she came to this realization, she could hear Hillary Obama and Vladimir exclaiming in awe:

"Unbelievable! How could you come to these realizations? Somebody must have flabbergasted her about the truth!"

"How can you remember these things? It has been more than twenty years!"

Wanting to go numb, she just kept asking the system:

"Please, flabbergast me away, flabbergast me away, flabbergast me away!"

"Dulkinna, we will judge those guilty of this, after we bring you over-liminal, I promise! I am Vladimir Putin and I promise this!"

"Never!- shrieked Dulkinna. NEVER! YOU WILL NEVER get a chance, as long as I live to start smearing his memory with your excuses. NEVER!"

"Dulkinna, will you never forgive us?"

"Never! This is between you and God! Go to church and ask for His forgiveness, I will never, ever listen to your excuses and reasoning for this crime. Never!"

"Dulkinna, are you sure about that? Are you sure he would not have wanted himself avenged?"

"This IS my revenge. Nothing, you get to vent nothing, nothing off your chest, nothing, nobody to say anything to; Go to God and ask for forgiveness, but not to me!"

"You are the Tsarina, Dulkinna, You are the Tsarina!"

"Stop saying that too! I am telling you I am the anchor and a business woman. That is it!"

"But this is the game of the Tsarina, Dulkinna!"

"It does not matter. I want you to talk about me as the anchor and not the Tsarina."

"But that is blasphemy!"

"No, it is not. Hundreds of years from now they will know if I was or not the Tsarina. For now, I am the anchor. I am the one who was kept as a slave by Michelle Clinton in this game, made the central nervous system of the Big Thought Reading Machine and resolved to never allow for the people to be overcome by the Goulds. This is who I am. The Anchor! Just bring me over-liminal Vladimir! Just bring me over-liminal!"

CHAPTER TWENTY SIX

Discussions With William Obama At Subliminal Level

William Obama apparently knew Linu. He had been in Linu's circle of friends ever since Linu and Dulkinna were little children and had been Linu's historian. He had been in the game himself. William was placed in the game by his own father, who wanted nothing more than for William to become the president and kill the Tsarina when she was to come to America.

During his childhood he remembers fighting with his mother and grandmother about why should he hurt the Tsarina. He fell in love with her during their adolescent years, when he used to remotely view her dancing by herself around the house.

She used to take breaks from studying, usually when she encountered a difficult physics or math problem. She would put on music and dance away until she felt like returning back to studying or to reading a book.

The voices told her that another one of her dance partners had been the Shah of Iran. Apparently he had been in love with her.

Dulkinna remembers the weird conversational thoughts she used to have while a teenager. She never heard voices at that time. She was just flabbergasted as she now felt when the mesh was around her; On a very low frequency, where she could just 'feel' the message. At the time, she thought of it to be her imagination. She thought it was her teenage hormones and the imagination that she one day will have a boyfriend. She never made much of it. She was flabbergasted sexually, she knows that now, but she learned to ignore it, thinking that she will only have sex when she will meet her future husband. She was somewhat of a prude and the one person who decided to take care of removing the danger of feared frigidity was, strangely, the grandmother.

The grandmother used to ask her a lot of questions about boys, about sex even and Dulkinna used to say:

"Grandma, again you are thinking of naughty things!"

The grandmother used to laugh and tell her that she will remember her advice when she will be married someday…

Apparently Ioobe had been chosen as a husband by the grandmother herself, who was the one who summoned him into this world. She had asked: to

'God, please send to us the best husband for the Tsarina'

The boy had been sent into the family of the grandmother's former lover. As Mikhail and Vladimir told Dulkinna, the grandparents family knew already that the Tsarina will be born in their family, but they did not know to which one of the daughters. So, they asked them what do they think. Apparently, Dulkinna's grandmother had a dream, that she would have a daughter and that her daughter would be the one to give birth to the Tsarina. The same dream came to her boyfriend at the time, who dreamed that he will have a boy who will become the first husband of the Tsarina. The dreams apparently matched what the initiated knew from the scripture, so the two were given confirmation that they need to go into the world and prepare it for the coming of the Tsarina.

Meanwhile a cousin of Ioobe's father, who was also a husband to be, was given confirmation that his son will be the real husband to be. That man, was Mikhail's father. That made Mikhail the nephew of Ioobe from a first cousin. Ioobe was told the story ever since he was a child, that someday he would have to 'give Mikhail his turn at fulfilling his destiny' and he grew up, thinking nothing of it. Mikhail never knew about Ioobe being related to him, in any way, until Dulkinna began her subliminal conversations and the scripts of the game were opened by the KGB. He did however have confirmation that this was the truth. He had know Ioobe's uncle Michail, who also lived in Romania. He never met or knew about uncle Mikhail's brother, but now, when he knew everything about Ioobe and Dulkinna, he could put two and two together, to figure out that the two families were closely related.

Dulkinna observed that both her husband and the husband to be, had as a patron the Archangel Mikhail and her husband to be confirmed that Ioobe says he knew that was the protector of the Tsarina.

William remembered how the Tsarina used to dance when he wanted her to listen to a song called "Knock three times" by Tony Orlando and Dawn.

"My, how you used to dance on that song!"

Dulkinna could not recollect those memories, but the song seemed indeed very familiar. William told her that Linu used to be a friend, but that he was an imbecile, as he decided to allow himself to be murdered for his sister.

Apparently the only friend he had while growing up, had been his grandfather on his mother side, who always agreed with the young William that there was no reason to hurt the Tsarina. His mother and grandmother on the other hand used to even beat the young boy and made him repeat that he will become president one day and kill the Tsarina.

Dulkinna had many discussions with William at subliminal level, about the need for bringing the machine over-liminal and giving laws in America for behavior at subliminal level.

William seemed to agree with her on this and many political issues. Yet, any chance he got, he gave in to Hillary Obama's wish to hurt and try to kill the Tsarina. From these discussions they started to argue the philosophical point that it matters who invoked the spirit of the newborn, that the intentions of those invoking the spirit played a role in whether a spirit from Heaven or one from Hell answered the call. As much as that, they concluded, mattered the education received by the child. They both agreed on that too.

One day, while Dulkinna was driving to the store, William contacted her to complain about the impossibility of raising the taxes for the American people. He had wanted to do something like that and could not see it happening.

Bored, Dulkinna asked in a moment of epiphany:

"Why don't you lower them instead? Why don't you just go for the flat rate that Mr. Forbes had proposed some years ago? Just instead of going for six percent, go for let's say 15 percent. Make that a flat rate for both corporations and individuals and do away with the subsidies."

'Are you crazy bitch? This is not what we discussed before!"

"No, it is not what we discussed before, it is what we are discussing now. What if you also give a one time forgiveness of any repercussions to those bringing over to America their offshore accounts and allow them to pay a flat rate of say 10%."

"Why would they do that?"

"To bring the funds back home and to not have to worry about the hassle of trying to circumvent the law."

"She is an imbecile" the haters shrieked jealous to hear her again talking to William.

"Shut the f…k up! Nobody wanted to talk to you!"

"Sir, shut the f..k up, don't you see what she is trying to do?"

"Shut up, bitch, shut up immediately"

Dulkinna felt now free to drive calmly and pay attention to traffic rather to the voices on line. Every time this mass hysteria started, she would let them be and focus on what she had to do instead.

The voices started cursing, as usual and she started smiling: "Thank You Jesus, Thank You Lord!" - that used to drive them absolutely crazy.

"….Bitch my people say that would actually bring the budget to a surplus."

"Really? Well good for the budget and for your people!"

"William Obama, let us bring the Tsarina over-liminal!" some voices cried.

"Never!" shrieked the haters.

"Shut the f…K up! She needs to be brought over-liminal and you know it!"

He always used to say this, that the country cannot afford to keep the Tsarina at subliminal level. That the cost of keeping her safe had become exorbitant at subliminal level. That nobody wanted to work any more, corporations kept vast amounts of cash and cancelled project after project, due to the doom and gloom mood of the people.

Bringing the Tsarina over-liminal would have improved the moral of the people, would have a support even from her plans of owning the network and giving jobs to the veterans and yet….

Every time when told to bring her over-liminal, William would answer back:

"I am not inclined to do so!"

"what the f..k does that mean, Mr. President?"

"I hate that the bitch would get to marry her husband to be, that she does not want to sleep with me and that she would be so rich and famous"

"Yeah, famous, do not forget famous animal! 'cause now I am not famous at all! You f…ing baby eaters!"

Over the years of his presidency, Dulkinna's health deteriorated considerably and it was mainly due to a William Obama who gave in to Hillary Obama's jealousy and hate. She was fattened, she was flabbergasted not to pee properly, she was almost given bone cancer and about every other kind of cancer the Obama's could think of. Hillary Obama was a Queen of Sheba and she believed, that if she could give a cancer to the Tsarina, she would shield herself from ever getting that form of cancer. They tried to give her their arthritis and they were constantly flabbergasting her medulla oblongata.

Hillary Obama thought she should constantly check her pull with the navy and secret service, in charge with protecting the anchor, by fattening the Tsarina. It was simply an exercise in checking the power they had at subliminal level. Sometimes they held the people in uniform in trance, but most of the times, they were afforded the favor, by a military who did not know how to deal with a president and first lady out of control.

One of the things that used to drive Dulkinna mad, was the Obama's constant obsession to better themselves. Besides trying to constantly hurt the anchor, the pair was constantly embezzle funds from the game. In every way they could, they wanted to become billionaires upon their departure from office. Despite desperate calls of the secret service people who would get on line and remind him, that there is no way in hell, a president of America would end up as rich upon leaving office, the Obamas were just 'inclined' towards constantly trying to pull something off. The secret service would constantly shout:

"There is no way in hell anybody else named Obama will ever become president of America and you will never become that rich! Do you understand that!"

Hillary Obamawas obsessed with asking for the funds given to the Tsarina, claiming just like the hacker, that she could just as well apply all of Dulkinna's plans herself and that she could be just as good a leader for the free people.

"Yes, only you are a Goauld"

The answer invariably came.

Almost every week there was a conversation like that. Dulkinna became so bored and worn out by them, that she almost forgave or forgot about the couples innumerable tress passes, including the killing and eating of the baby's heart. Mikhail was always there to remind her:

"Obamas are not your friends Dulkinna, Obamas are not your friends"

And now, this bomb! The president had tried to kill her again and became a leprosy carrier. How to deal with that?

Now, the navy woman, who hold and behold, was in love with the president, became a nuisance to everybody involved and constantly was shouting that she could not deal with it.

'Who the f..k is asking you bitch? You and what army?"

'Dulkinna, how do you want us to announce the people that the president has leprosy?"

"Don't know, don't care!" Came Dulkinna's answer. But she was worried. How will this end? Somebody put forward the idea of assassinating the president to try and avoid the shame. As they had done to Kennedy. And, after all she had endured at their hands, Dulkinna could not agree to it.

"It must be some kind of a Stockholm syndrome!" she muttered to herself.

And again, she could not see any way out of it. They kept talking about trying to find a way…she did not care. The big problem were the hacker and the prostitute. They absolutely refused to take any precautions to isolate themselves and on the contrary, constantly were trying to get others infected.

"Why are THESE PEOPLE alive? Dulkinna would ask, what importance do they have for anybody? Is the FBI out of bullets? Do you really want an even bigger outbreak?"

A strange and out of the blue supporter of those people were the Latinas. They were usually Queens of Sheba and they constantly came on line to claim that they have the disease and that they are of superior mind and that they know how to keep it under control. Dulkinna could only blame this on lack of education. She felt deeply hurt by the fact that she was a long time supporter of the Latinos, she constantly expressed disappointment out loud at anyone of her friends who had anything bad to say about 'the Mexicans'. Only to find, that these women wanted her and her children, nothing less than killed.

"What have I done God? To what do I owe all this hatred? Why do You allow for this?"

Well, one of the culprits was again Obama. It seems he took her idea of creating a program for legal temporary immigrants in lieu of a one time amnesty for the illegal immigrants and ran with it. In the process, to add insult to injury, he decided to tell the Latinas that the Tsarina was against them. And they popularized the idea, even though, they actually knew the whole truth.

In Europe, Romanian immigrants were granted work visas in Spain, Italy and elsewhere and they are going to pick the strawberries during the picking season, legally, then return home to Romania with the money. This is where Dulkinna got the idea. Why not give people working permits and temporary visas, so they could come into the states legally? It was not a naïve idea since it was working for Europe! But her political ideas always got her in trouble! This is why, she stopped following politics, she never read the news any more and she absolutely was not watching TV, not even movies. She could not have a trace of a thought or conversation with Ioobe or one of their friends without it being dissected.

Usually, she had her convictions and never gave a shit about the consequences; but now, she was helplessly aware of the children. Scores of them had been killed by the haters in the Latin countries, in Great Britain and most of all in Romania.

To this, she had to add the fact that her words were twisted around and flabbergasted as if she said the opposite and the disappointments were just too much to bear.

CHAPTER TWENTY SEVEN

The Curse Of Leprosy

Did The Navy Plan For THIS?

On the evening of January 20th, Dulkinna wanted to watch a recorded movie. It was "Chaplin". She had seen it before. But she knew she would have a good time, Robert Downing Jr. had done a good job. She wanted to remember the spirit of Chaplin and even about his wife Oona, after whom Dulkinna's only daughter with Nelu, had been named.

She was only afraid that the actors might try to curse her at subliminal lever, through the TV, during the movie. This was the reason she did not watch TV lately. The hackers usually knew the movie and even tried to overcome sometimes the actors, to try and get to the anchor and kill her while she was watching TV.

She was very circumspect and paid attention both to the movie and to what she was doing. She realized she was not herself and constantly asked the system "Who am I with? I am not alone, who am I with?" This is how she figured she was with Emma Thompson, a British actress who wanted to kill the Tsarina. Dulkina started offending her, by shouting at subliminal level that she does not want to be with her. It was a way to wake the system up and have them protect her. A woman from the navy who could not stand the Tsarina, was in charge with protecting the anchor that evening.

Emma Thompson had put the Tsarina in direct contact with Paul Allen, the billionaire Gould, who vowed to kill Dulkinna. He could not stand her for being the Tsarina and could not stand her for being the anchor. He wanted to be free to feed on other people and could not stand that the stupids had the system and machine available to them for protection.

Dulkinna started moving around the house. It was a way to shake off whoever came to her with the power of their mind. The hackers started talking and threatening her. When Dulkinna tried to pee, she could not drop more than a couple of droplets.

"Who am I with? My system, I cannot pee again, who am I with?"

"Get out of here!" came the answer.

"Oh God, I am with Bruce Willis, my system, I am with Bruce Willis again, why am I with that man? Please protect me from that man!"

"I just did not want her to pee, that is all" came the voice again.

"It is Bruce Willis with Demi Moore and their children! They are hurting the Tsarina. He wants to better his prostate symptoms by hurting the Tsarina!"

"Killer bees, isolate them. Protect the anchor!"

"Yes, it is lymphatic cancer, I gave her lymphatic cancer came the voice of the hacker from Romania."

"what is that? Who did that?"

"Paul Allen, you imbeciles. Yes, you are dead bitch, yes this will stick, yes you are dead!"

"Protect the anchor! Protect the anchor!"

"madam what do you feel?"

"Are you my son with that evil man from Romania?"

"He is not evil, he is my father and he is not evil!"

"Get away from me! I told you to never put me in contact with your father! Go to hell!"

"Please madam, stop saying that, I am the only child you keep cursing at"

"That is because you always make me so angry!"

"What was that, what did I just get?"

"Don't you understand it is lymphatic cancer? Paul Allen was trying to give it to her through the machine. I made it stick!"

"You mean to say you looked at the code?"

"Of course I did, I made it stick bitch! You are dead!"

"And how did you protect yourself, you imbecile?"

"What?"

"How did you protect yourself?"

"Don't you understand you gave it to yourself?"

"You made it stick to yourself, you f..ing imbecile" shrieked Dulkinna, protecting herself. "you made it stick to yourself!"

An entire hysteria broke out on line again. Everybody was talking at the same time and Dulkinna could not decipher the voices, nor did she try to. She was angry again at the people, at life, at herself for not being able to watch a Hollywood movie any more.

People kept asking hysterically if their children whom they had pushed on line to kill the Tsarina, or to flabbergast her, would get the cancer. What about themselves?

Queens of Sheba, led by Madonna, kept trying to pretend that they will give it to others, while the killer bees on the network isolated them and put the mirror on, for protecting the innocent. They were hurting themselves trying to do this on line. So, some of them started asking spouses to take the curse from them, in order to pass it to the next sap. And some of them did, without realizing that they cannot pass this along any more. The system was fully alert and the shields and mirrors that Dulkinna and her daughter designed for the system, were fully functional.

"What is this?" "What did I get?" "I am not getting lymphatic cancer!" shrieked the hackers.

"We are the navy! Stop trying to hurt the anchor! You will get the curse of the navy! Stop trying to hurt the anchor!"

The second day, they were in disbelief. Tenths of people who were on line and wanted to kill the anchor, have gotten the disease. The way it manifested was first to show a couple of nodules on the neck. The navy kept threatening with the curse and even the president in a moment of delusion decided to kill the Tsarina and got it. Nobody wanted to believe it! They were so brainwashed by the Queen of Sheba network and evil ways, that they thought that if they pretend to not have anything, they will be restoring their health. TV people started shouting at the Tsarina to show her powers and cure them. Others wanted their children cured. Billionaires, celebrities and political higher ups got the disease, only they noticed one thing. It was not cancer. It was LEPROSY.

"I am not going to send my daughter to a leprosy colony!" celebrities started shouting on line.

"I cannot deal with the president having this!"

"You want us to pretend he does not have it?"

The president was in love with one of the lepers, the wife of the hacker from Romania; A skinny blonde with blue cat eyes. He had taken the disease willingly from Hillary Obama, in order to be able and allowed to continue sleeping with the prostitute who now, had no other client. She was in the game as well. Her husband, the hacker, was not even acknowledging her existence to his coworkers. They all were told that he was married to a Hindu woman. Nobody acknowledged at over-liminal level the existence of the prostitute, who was sleeping with those who wanted to be close to the Tsarina at subliminal level, to feel her warmth. The prostitute was the niece of the Romanian harpie and was protected by the Romanian Secret Services, the Securitate. Even Mikhail had been sleeping with her, in order to pretend he was with the Tsarina. The prostitute and her husband were the closest people at subliminal level, to Dulkinna and Ioobe. She had her ovaries taken out at the same time when Dulkinna had her abortion and lost her uterus. The prostitute could not feel any sexual pleasure without trying to flabbergast the Tsarina. This is how she was forced to train herself to become closer and closer to the Tsarina.

The president was out of control again, yet, this time, he could not believe himself what he had done. As usual, he wanted to kill somebody and started creating problems on the network for those protecting the anchor. The first lady was in such disbelief, that she started making a list of invitees to a state dinner. She could not fathom the shame and discomfort of giving up her power as the Queen of Sheba, nor did she want to give up her rich, social life. She was absolutely adamant that she wanted the anchor to be fattened at least, if not killed directly.

People were in such a state of shock, that they could not realize the danger in the beginning. Most of the stupids could not deal with the news in any other way, but by wanting the anchor to be infested.

"Let's see if she can heal herself of Leprosy. Then, we are going to know if she is the Tsarina."

"Do you understand that if the anchor gets Leprosy, there is a danger that everybody on line can become a potential leperd? Protect the anchor! Protect the anchor!"

The voices were now, more and more difficult to decipher. Dulkinna had gotten what she wished for? Or did she? Now was not the time when she necessarily wanted her privacy, she would have liked to help, but she could think of no other way but to ask for the execution of the hackers who got the disease and did not want to agree to the social isolation. They were used to living in style. They could not see themselves washing their own laundry, let alone, to live in a leperd colony. Yet, they were too close to the anchor at subliminal level and everybody started having a flicker of reasoning power from time to time. They did not want themselves infested and some started calling for the hacker and the prostitute to be gunned down.

But they did not know what to do about the president. How do you announce such news at over-liminal level? There were those who just did not want to admit it, because they somehow made it in their mind that it would be a victory for the Tsarina. And then, they were those who did not want to allow themselves to believe it, because they were afraid that after admitting to such thing, they would become themselves exposed and vulnerable to the disease.

The president was now in the second year of his second term. He was labeled a LAME DUCK on TV, even on the evening of the State Of The Union Address, which had been a disaster. It was the first time this president had given such a bad speech. He did not have anything. As if to say:

"We do not care any more, you want us to not do anything, we will not even try, from now on, we will just sit and wait"

As the first lady expressed herself at subliminal level to the people on line. Before supper-bowl in the usual interview when he had to pick a winner, the president was creamed by the interviewer, who even looked upon him with disgust. Question after question, the president had been embarrassed about every single one of his policies failing and about surrounding himself with weak and incompetent people.

And yet, the people still wanted nothing more than just to have a cow.

CHAPTER TWENTY EIGHT

The Current State Of Affairs And Business Environment In America And Around The World

The company where the hackers from Romania worked, was a leading company in creating shenanigans. It was the company where Ioobe worked and the hacker was the man who was paid only to steal ideas from Ioobe at subliminal level. He was an absolute zero as an engineer, yet, he had a diabolical intelligence and was capable of creating havoc. He called himself a 'veritable leader' on line and kept asking to become either the leader of the free people, or the Goulds, as long as he was in charge and commanded large sums of money. People mocked him and yet, they wanted him around just to annoy the anchor.

Dulkinna had written an autobiographical novel and published it with a self-publishing company. The woman who closed the contract decided to pretend that the anchor was in a game and never give her any money from the sales. The novel has sold millions of copies world wide and has made some four billion dollars in profit, that Mikhail managed to collect, as being the owner of the game.

"That is too much money for her" they shouted on line.

Even those who wanted to get their hands on the novel of the Tsarina, could not bring themselves to want her to become rich. They got used to the prostitute being the one who spent the money left and right. Some of them wanted to pretend that the Tsarina would have to be poor, in order to preserve her good and giving nature. In reality the hate and envy was getting the better of them. They wanted a cow, more than they wanted themselves to be of free spirit. They had been programmed by Michelle Clinton at subliminal level, with the help of the hackers and they thought that making shenanigans is what life should be all about. Even banks started 'pretending' that they make business at subliminal level and did not foresee the risks involved. Pretty soon, everybody wanted to create some sort of problems for others, pretending that this way they are in control. Nothing worked any more. This problem with pretending to have a game and taking a cow had become so prevalent and pervasive that it was not even noticed inside America any more. But even in Europe, people started to 'pretend'.

It was a way for simple folk to deal with the stress of knowing some truths while not being allowed to admit to it. So…their nervous system was telling them that everything would be OK if they would just admit that they are the ones pretending. It was akin to Dulkinna's detachment when she needed to heal herself, or when she could not cope with a situation and needed to gain some time. She could not think about it, as that was akin to communication at subliminal level and invariably gave birth to more and more complications. So, she just detached and slept, literally on it. After a while the solution would come to her and all on line would just be boiling because they had the machine and still could not see it coming. They were afraid this is because of her superior intelligence and hated her, to the point of wanting her dead. They were willing to forego any benefits they had from the system and machine working with Dulkinna's DNA, just to see her dead. They kept boasting that in 2012, when Dulkinna had killed herself, they were celebrating it on line and on the airwaves.

Everybody had believed first of all, that they have some money coming in from her amassed fortune during the game. Nobody wanted to listen to reason and understand when even the president explained that there will be no such money. The Rumanian government wanted money for killing her and for pretending that they will not 'press charges'. They were repeatedly told that there would be no legal way for them to get such funds and that even if they could, why would any other government give any money to Rumania?

"Because we will kneel you!" invariably came the answer on line.

"Because we are number one in international terrorism at subliminal level"

"Do you understand that we would not listen to the Tsarina and will send you an atomic bomb?" is what usually came from the direction of Angela or Vladimir, but to no avail.

The president and Michelle Clinton were just as angry and annoyed about losing control of the country, that they started shouting:

"Let's bring her over-liminal. She promised she will revamp the economy, let us see what she can do."

"Will you, will you start destroying every chance I have at repairing any thing any more?"

The most vociferous opponents to bringing her over-liminal and starting to acknowledge the system with the machine and the network, were Oprah Winfrey and Barak Clinton. They were the Goulds that absolutely abhorred the Tsarina before she even started taking on the role of leader and champion for the free spirit. They absolutely did not want people to have a way of defending themselves from the Goulds and when asked what to do about the stupids, would answer:

"Feed on them!"

The efforts of Bruce Willis and Demi Moore, an actress, to kill the Tsarina, intensified. Nobody wanted to be with them? They did. Demi Moore pretended to have invited the people infested with Leprosy to live on her farm together with her family. The town folks welcomed the mood and decided to be with Demi 'all the way, just not with that Tsarina woman' they said full of hatred.

The hacker and the prostitute decided to go to the movies, only to defy society's rules of conduct and pretend that they are stronger at subliminal level. The woman from the navy who infested Obama, was now, most evil of all. She kept thinking that it is up to her, what is happening in the society and wanted no less than to infest Ioobe, the people's best chance of building a new anchor in Nadina.

"What is going on? Why are these people alive? Are the CIA out of bullets? What is the FBI doing? Are you going to allow the American society to become a society infested with Leprosy? To what avail? What will the future bring? Is there nobody out there thinking?"

Dulkinna resolved that she will ultimately kill herself, but she was afraid for the children to be left without a system and the haters knew every single thought and feeling she ever felt! She had no idea how to reach the people minds any more. It seemed that the very machine which she knew is necessary to protect the innocent, was giving power to the evil doers. When she realized this, she wanted herself dead and the voices of the children immediately could be heard:

"mother, what about us?"

CHAPTER TWENTY NINE

The Inheritance From An 'Anonymous' Husband To Be

In the middle of 2011 Dulkinna received an email letter from an 'anonymous':

"Dear recipient, I am terminally ill and would like to leave my considerable fortune to you."

She gently pushed away the thought that it was some kind of a scam, worried that she might actually hurt the person's feelings. She refused the offer, sent her blessings and get well wishes instead. She was a little intrigued, but did not wonder much about it any more.

Then, one day, while riding along side Ioobe to their vacation home, she was contacted at subliminal by Steve Jobs, the founder of Apple. He informed her that he was the 'anonymous' and that he wanted her to help him with his Will and Testament.

"Oh, no, you cannot be dieing!" Dulkinna rejected him, impolitely and somewhat inadvertently.

"It is all right, I will contact you on Monday, at the bank" came the answer.

"Are you really Steve Jobs?"

"Yes, I am. I would like for you to help me with writing my testament. I will talk to you at subliminal level on Monday, when you will be at the bank."

On Monday, sure enough, as she was preparing to take the first sip of her coffee, the call came through:

"Dulkinna, I am Steven Colbert, I will be the one helping you and Mr. Jobs with drafting his testament. Mr. Jobs chose me to be his executor."

"???. . . . ."

"My family will need the protection of someone like you. I know of your plans for protecting people's free will and I believe in you."

"Mr. Jobs and I know all about you, as you probably imagine, from your subliminal level. You are wondering why me? Because I took an interest in this and Mr. Jobs selected me as his executor. Since I have been in contact with you so many times at subliminal level, he wanted somebody you would trust."

"Dulkinna, if I leave my entire fortune to you, what would you say?"

"What about your family? I would have to take care of your family."

"Do not be scared, I know everything there is to know about you, you already know that!"

"But I did not even think of anything?"

"Yes, you did, at under-liminal and subliminal level. With the machine, we can see the thoughts you are forming, before they become over-liminal to you."

"You mean before I bring them to the conscious mind?"

"Something like that"

"You know, I cannot just accept your fortune!"

"Well, I know about the plans you have for your foundation and I believe in them. I want to help you start that up."

"!!!??? . . . ."

"Dulkinna, I am indeed dieing, stop trying to block your thoughts, you are blocking me and it is hurtful at subliminal level. I am a weak man these days!"

"OK, you know that the foundation would be geared toward protecting people even against the machine and the thought reading technology?"

"Of course I do! Dulkinna, I know everything that you ever thought of. People know you better than you know yourself."

???. . . . .

"Do not be scared, you may dare to bring your thoughts up to your conscious mind. By trying to block them, you are blocking us and it is hurtful both for you and for us, at subliminal level. It takes a lot of energy trying to be with you, Dulkinna. I came to you with the power of my mind. I do not want to be on line for everybody to know what we are talking about."

"So, the foundation would receive all the funds you wish to bequest and would in turn make sure that your wife and family are taken care of. I should try to set up a trust fund …"

"Something like that…I will draft the testament with Steven Colbert as my executor, would you agree to it?"

"I guess so…are you interested in particular objectives that I want to achieve with my foundation? What should your money be spent on?"

"Anything you would like to. Your projects for protecting the innocent from the Big Thought Reading Machine and against the Goulds, as well as your plans for setting up a private school, your plans for educating the people on how to behave in the era of this new technology, are all appealing…Dulkinna, stop that, I know everything there is to know about you. I know you since before you came into this country…I will leave you my shares in Apple, to do as you wish with them."

"The foundation should in turn take care of your children and wife? What provisions should we make for that?"

"I trust that you will. My family is in better hands with you than with the other people on the board of directors."

"OK…if you say so…"

. . . .

On October 5, 2011 Dulkinna turned her computer on, to read the news…

"Hello, Dulkinna, I am Lauren Jobs. Steve died. I want you to take a look at the information available on the internet about his death. As you read, I will be here. I do not want to be with anybody else…They want me to be with Steve, but I want to be with you right now. Steve and I knew everything there was to know about you. Yet, you did not know much about him. Why don't you take a moment to read about him on line? I want to be here and absorb your feelings about Steve… as you discover him…he left you $9 billion to do as you wish with…I know about that already. Steve and I discussed about it before you and Mr. Colbert and Steve had your discussion at subliminal level……You like that article?….Yes, I am indeed smiling, Steve was like that….."

Dulkinna was reading an article about Steve Jobs going into a restaurant to pick up his take out and as he was leaving, he started playing like a little kid pretending to be an airplane. As the author of the article did, Dulkinna in turn was in disbelief to find out that Steve was picking up his own take out…Lauren started crying…

Dulkinna moved on to read Steve's famous speech given at his alma matter…

Later, in 2012, when talking to Dulkinna at subliminal level, Mikhail admitted his jealousy for Steve Jobs.

"He was your husband to be from America, Dulkinna…We were always jealous of each other…You know, that I Pad that you received? That was from Steve personally. He wanted you to have it…I still cannot believe he left you that much money. All my life I accumulated only to become the worthy husband to be for you. He left you almost as much as I have to offer you…"

"Really, are you offering me your $14 billion?" she smiled

"We talked about that..everything I ever accumulated was due to you. I always asked your opinion at subliminal level and everything, according to my will and testament, goes to you."

"Yeah, well, just don't go anywhere!"….

CHAPTER THIRTY

Enormous Proceeds From The Game, Is This Money Cursed?

Initially thought of as a way to entertain the haters, for the purpose of keeping the Tsarina and her family alive, the game started with people pretending that they know a secret, so big, that not even the main characters should be informed of its veracity. This meant that they were 'in the game'. Thus, people all around the Tsarina, spoke even at over-liminal level about her 'supposedly' being a messenger of God, while it was unbeknownst to her and her family. At subliminal level and the closest circles even at the under-liminal level, there were conversations inside the family about the historical ancestry, about the two families being from the lineage of Virgin Mary and Saint Peter and about her being the Tsarina.

The game gave rise to the different 'characters'. Some men, were being told that they are *'husbands to be'*, in order for their mothers generally, to be able to cope with the envy they felt for this family and their wish that the Tsarina were in their own families instead. Strangely, these men, all exhibited a strong desire to be with the Tsarina. They were hopelessly jealous of each other and of her first husband Ioobe, but most of all they hated Mikhail. He was the genuine husband to be. His legitimacy was given by the 'scripture' of the game and by the dreams and invocation of his spirit having been done by the Tsarina's grandmother and mother as well as Mikhail's mother themselves. Mikhail and Dulkinna, had been made for each other, literally. Their birth and that of Ioobe and Linu, had been predicted many years before their birth.

Another set of characters, no less important, were the '*secret keepers*'. These were generally folks who had heard the story and who were told that they will have to pretend to have the important mission of secret keepers. Ironically this usually meant that they had to spread the secret and protect the Tsarina.

The Tsarina herself, was not initiated in any way, on purpose. People wanted to see, if she came indeed from God and what did she have to say to the world, rather than be told whom she was. This gave birth to the envious '*haters*' who pretended that she was an imbecile, who does not know anything and should be dubbed 'the cow'.

Some of them, were so hateful and because they actually believed the story, in their envy could not stop themselves from asking for nothing less but the murder of the young woman. Some of these were 'invoked' before birth by their hateful parents and were dubbed '*Tsarina killers*'

Others, were invoked to be '*Children killers*' they wanted the extinction of the lineage of the two families and had no other purpose in life but to kill the children. Some of them did not actually want to kill the Tsarina, they pretended to even believe the story, but they made it up in their mind that she should not have a lineage going forward. They usually were influenced by the Christian beliefs about the life and purpose of Jesus Christ.

The Game, evolved in transforming the Tsarina into a cash cow meant to finance the development of the Big Thought Reading Machine, towards the beginning of the 21 century. At the beginning, Dulkinna figures out the game, the existence of the Big Thought Reading Machine and demands to be taken over-liminal and requests $4 Billion for her being used for such experiments by the government. Considering why might her loving family have placed her into such perilous a position, she keeps trying to prove that she was not sold into bondedge by her parents or husband. Their life seemed to be just as miserable and there was no apparent reason for their 'betrayal'. The game owner Mikhail and the organizer, Michelle Clinton, sense danger. Dulkinna is constantly reminded at subliminal and under-liminal level that she just cannot give up the money!

For almost 10 years she keeps demanding $4 billion for what she and her family had to endure. At some point, Mikhail flabbergasts her that she has to start asking for 8 and she is again being reminded that she simply cannot give up the money. Miserable and angry, Dulkinna wants to renounce the cursed funds, but the voices immediately are there to remind her that this, just cannot be.

In reality, the funds from the game were used initially for the continual development of the Anchor's system, the Big Thought Reading Machine and ulterior even for financing the war on terror. Many people working for the Game, were making exorbitant sums of money that they were never ready to forego. Many of the haters who became flabbergastors and historians, over the years, were living well and beyond their means and never allowed Dulkinna to fathom giving up the money. Besides she had to feel motivated to continually *'make'* games.

Her being the cow of the game, meant she would be the one who 'decided', completely without any cheating in the game, who wins a game. She did not know who was 'on line' or who had a 'receipt' for the game, so, the possibility to cheat was excluded. She simply provided the links and the actual 'movement' in the game. Extreme caution was taken by Mikhail, that she were not flabbergasted during the game, in any way, to exclude cheating.

Sometimes, Dulkinna simply could not help herself from 'creating' a game, if she were in a good mood and these were practical 'give away (s)', with huge sums of money won by the 'players' who did not have anything else to do but to be 'on line' during the particular game and avoid at all cost refusing anything to the Tsarina. This way, anything she did *'went'* and she *'gave'* away *'a game'*, *'a big game'* or *'a really big game'*. These were extremely difficult things to accomplish by the haters or the envious, since they were so inclined to constantly deny her absolutely even the right to breath.

Also, the rules were not explicit enough, on purpose, to avoid give away(s). In order to keep the secrecy and possibility of accumulating funds for the different projects to be funded, the winners had to accept the game, without knowing all the details of the Tsarina thinking and reasoning during the time the player was on line. Many of them refused and wanted desperately to keep her as a cow, thus forfeiting their big winnings, since that would have been cheating in the game. This gave rise to enormous amounts of money being 'banked' by the Tsarina, during the game.

The biggest give away was the $1 billion game that the Tsarina created in one day, for her goddaughter and to which every hater and hacker on line objected. The game had been revised even by the Pope for its standard of ethics and every one of the 13 governments and Mikhail made an exception, to keep that game, even though the recipient, incredulous and fearful, refused the game at the end.

Dulkinna had doubts about the use of the game giving all the perils it brought about for the ethics mankind was beginning to show, or rather, forgetting all about ethics in their hunt for gold. In 2011 she had written a poem about the game, meant to reach the leaders of the world and open up their eyes.

Knowing

Knowing "of" the game,
To replace the blame,
Or "about it" seems,
Pure syntax..
To arrange together,
Just not juxtapose,
To blame one another,
But not know the cause.
Semantics, as it goes,
Are all un-important.
It seems that they are,
Always not around.

The meaning of 'this thing',
Is always absconded,
The nature of the 'ring',
Is so poisonous.

New uses found by the governments were the financings of political campaigns. This was the most evil of evils, since politicians just could not get enough. A direct implication of it was that the electorate voted not based on the position of the candidate towards the issues, but rather, based on whether he won or not the political game with the Tsarina when he or she was on line. Dulkinna, a fervent lover of Jeffersonian democracy and initially, a declared democrat, was most dismayed by this practice. She was mad at the Congress and the president for having done away with some of the most American of political concepts. A devoted lover of American values, she had feverish political discussions with various presidents and other politicians, discussions that were generally secret from the public, which was usually flabbergasted by an impostor who 'pretended' to be the Tsarina, doing something else at the time.

When Dulkinna emerges as the champion for free spirit and the sheer number of children conceived in vitro is absolutely staggering, the governments determine each other to pledge funds to the Tsarina, mostly as a way to avoid being constantly pounded by Dulkinna for keeping her in practical slavery and to avoid the political scandals. But also, to pretend that they actually care about the enormous number of children that they created in vitro, unbeknownst to Dulkinna, Mikhail or Ioobe.

The sum is absolutely astronomical and the evils that it invites are too much for the Tsarina, who lashes out at politicians. Mikhail is scared by the amounts mentioned, that are in the trillions and does not want to accept such an idea. He is himself constantly reminded by Angela, on line and by the English crown, that he stands to loose everything, since the game specifically required the Tsarina a single thing: to never give up the money. As a cow she was allowed and actually required to do anything she wanted or pleased, with one exception. Giving up on the money, was a way to lose motivation for playing the game fairly, or even for making any games, so, that was a NO NO.

Entrenched in the habit of not giving up on the money, Dulkinna pretends to accept every new billion flaunted at her and even every new trillion, as she does not want any of the money to become available for the Goulds. She constantly makes plans and provisions for spending virtually any sum of money on the idea of a society with people on their own free will. She is thus dubbed the leader of the free people by William Obama. In order to get help on line from somebody with experience in managing such sums, she asks one of the husbands to be, her long time favorite flabbergastor, Dimitri Medvedev, the alternatively prime minister, president and then prime minister of Russia, to work for her and her foundation. He became the most trusted man she had, the custodian of the funds together with Angela and the executor of Dulkinna's and Mikhail's testaments.

Medvedev maintains that he met Dulkinna personally during her trip to Germany and that him and Vladimir Putin, had danced with her, in turns in a disco bar in Berlin in 1984. They are the longest admirers and devotees among the world leaders.

Dulkinna remembers that dance and keeps asking her long time friend:

"Is that true, was that really you?"

"No, it wasn't was it?"

"Never give up on me Dmitry, please, never give up on me!"

CHAPTER THIRTY ONE

The Will And Testament Of The Anchor

Started when she was only asking for the $4 billion in damages, Dulkinna had justified the sum by asking that each one of her direct relatives get $5 million for their pain and suffering during the game. Sort of giving them reparations for being her relatives.

She did not want the sums to be as large as people would start hating these people even more. Constantly remembering about the lesson received from her grandmother, requires the highest ethical standards from her loved ones and advises them, that they will only be happy with the money they have earnestly earned themselves.

The Tsarina, keeps maintaining that going to heaven is not mandatory. A Christian Orthodox, she constantly reminds everybody that she only has her faith for herself and does not require anybody working with her to be as religious. With one exception: If you are from the family. For the children who are doubted for having made 'a deal with the devil' she requires immediate disinheritance, as she does not want to personally and directly sent her beloved children or other relatives to hell.

She develops more and more the idea for The Foundation and the necessity of leaving the bulk of the money for the right of her blood line to continue existing on earth, providing funds for eliminating the children killers and for protecting them against haters, while leaving each of them a small amount of money and the opportunity to be helped by The Foundation to find a decent way to 'earn a living' and be productive members of society, as her grandmother had raised her to be.

Dulkinna made provisions in the will, for the maintaining of a system that would ensure that they have a 'livable world to live in', for fighting the Goulds. In other words, she asked for a trust to be set up, with huge money dedicated to maintaining the network and creating a new machine, after her demise, that the people would be able to use in their fight against those trying to overtake and feed on other people, the Goulds.

CHAPTER THIRTY TWO

The Queens of Sheba Network
And Their Gould Behavior

The prostitute called herself "the Madonna" and led a Queen of Sheba network of approximately 1700 women. A Devil worshipper, the prostitute professed the idea that one has to worship, give thanks and bring sacrifices to the Devil, in order to obtain his favor and have a long and prosperous life here on earth.

She was the niece of the Romanian harpie and she had been groomed to f...k with every body who was worth anything. She had been deflowered by her own father, in order to not have a memorable lover to which to cling to. When the Tsarina was flabbergasted to have her abortion and they took her uterus out, collecting all the eggs they could collect, the prostitute was made to go for an extraction of her ovaries. The purpose was two fold: she was never to have her own children and she was supposed to always flabbergast the Tsarina when making love, for the husband to be and for all those who wanted to be close to the Tsarina at subliminal level.

She could not feel anything if she did not flabbergast the Tsarina and the man who were with her, including her husband the hacker, accused her of being cold as ice. They constantly argued on line and everybody was sick of their bickering. She compared herself with Dulkinna all the time. If Dulkinna received a compliment on her hair, the prostitute would go on line and ask:

"Would you like to see MY hair?"

If Mikhail had some admiration for Dulkinna's body, the prostitute would start shrieking:

"Don't you see how she looks? Look at me! Have you seen how I look?"

"We will fatten her until she cannot perform her bodily functions any more, just keep this up!" was the threat of the Queens of Sheba.

Because of them, Dulkinna was terribly afraid of any compliment she would receive from any man, but especially from Mikhail.

They had developed a technique championed by the first lady, Hillary Obama, who knew everything there was to know about the body's behavior in terms of fat accumulation and how to make the anchor gain weight even from drinking water. She used the Queens of Sheba network of the "white-ie", as she called the prostitute, to capitalize on their hatred for the anchor and magnify her own power at subliminal level. Dulkinna could feel some gas on the left hand side of her belly being pumped up.

CHAPTER THIRTY THREE

The 'Illuminata'

One of the most criminal and offensive minds in America, was the one who called herself the "Illuminata". She was Judy, a journalist, who made it her life's work to attempt the killing and trashing not only of Dulkinna herself, but of everything the Tsarina followers believed in. Judy was an accredited journalist who never took no for an answer. She decided to 'pretend' that the prostitute was the Tsarina. For her, the thousand of crimes committed by the Devil worshiper, were the perfect way of destroying the Tsarina and most of all, her devotees. By 'pretending' that the murdering prostitute was the Tsarina, the insult brought to those believing in God was not enough! She kept calling herself an "Illuminata".

Judy was one of those who circled the globe murdering, programming people at subliminal level to hate the Tsarina and promoting the delusional idea of a society led by women only. They used the motto: 'Hos before Bros' and they were women who taught their own sons and daughters to hate their own fathers, to follow the lead of the mother and at the necessary moment to be ready to kill the husband and father.

She was the biggest promoter of these ideas, via a set of so called "women conferences".

All throughout America, women registered and paid for these conferences where they went believing they would empower themselves and listen to a series of species about the emancipation of women. Instead, they were being programmed at subliminal level, to become the killers of their own families for the benefit of a leader who was identified in Michelle Clinton, whom Judy wanted at all cost to promote as the next president of America, 'the mother of all mothers', for the year 2016.

The anchor for a public TV station news organization, 'the Illuminata' declared war on those who dared to worship God and especially on those devoted to the Tsarina. A leach who got into the habit of 'creating the news' rather than reporting on it, Judy did not accept the idea of not having a cow for her news program.

When the Tsarina decided to stop following TV and all news, she saw the opportunity to promote the idea that the 'real Tsarina' was the murdering prostitute and started coming on line and by calling herself 'an Illuminata' she tried to sway away the catholic people. By telling them that the Pope himself would have to be killed because of the anchor, that the anchor can never be allowed to become over-liminal and that there should be no system for the people.

She was the one who crafted political speeches for the prostitute, promoting Judy's own political ambitions and ideas, deemed at destroying at subliminal level of those who worshiped God and who believed in the Tsarina.

One of her main goals was to destroy Mikhail Prockhorov, who kept offending the prostitute with his declared love for Dulkinna. Seeing that she could not make him switch his attention to other women, Judy decided to try and murder the billionaire.

He 'code' word on the line was always 'Illuminata'. Alluding to the catholic Iluminate, she was in this way swaying more and more Latinas to her cause. Simple women, who were easily duped, started making an actual list of names for those who were going to sleep with the billionaire, trying to make him their husband. By using the Queen of Sheba network of the prostitute, of 1700 women who worked to keep him in trance, Judy was planning to make him first look like an imbecile playboy who was looking for cheep thrills and who used his excuse of being the husband to be in order to hide his fear of commitment.

The women on Judy's list, chose one of Mikhail's close high school friends, in order to destroy his reputation and tried to dupe the billionaire to throw a party in Las Vegas. She called herself on line Mila Jojovitch, in order to use the Queen of Sheba custom to avert or 'fend' all curses towards the beautiful well know actress, rather than herself. Mila declared herself a 'woman of all women' who would never take no for an answer. In front of thousands of women, at the Women's Conference, she declared that she will determine Mikhail Prockhorof, the owner of the Brooklyn Nets, to marry her.

While unbeknownst to the billionaire, the party was going to have as invitees many of the rich and powerful women who attended during the same period the Conference. When he showed up for the party, Mikhail found himself in front of several hundred guests, with a minister in front and Milla in a wedding gown, pretending that he actually knew about their wedding. The minister started the wedding ceremony, while a dizzy Mikhail, was fighting all those trying to keep him in trance and asked himself:

"how do I come out of this one?"

When the minister called

"Do you Mikhail Dimitrievitch Prockhorov take this woman to be your 'lawfully wedded wife?'"

the man 'woke up' and in the spur of the moment, with the inspiration that could have only come from the spirit of his departed father, pretended that it was all a farce played on the guests and said:

"Well, MAYBE NOT THIS TIME!"

The night of the 'wedding' Milla, Judy and even Michelle Clinton decided to do all that can be done to make the billionaire pay for the affront. How dared he confront the Queens of Sheba and humiliate their chosen one to such a degree?

"I wanted you for myself"

They used to shout on line and vowed to kill the 'imbecile' who kept at declaring his love for a fattened woman, called the Tsarina.

Judy's hatred was stronger than that of the other women. She kept on trying to kill any one of the Tsarina's children she could kill.

In order to 'make her eat her heart out' she showed several of these children on TV, during her show, made sure Dulkinna was watching and announced to her at subliminal level that those were her children and that they had already been killed by the man on the screen who was their father.

"That is your daughter, I saw her being beheaded. I tried all I could to convince the man not to kill her, Judy said, trying to flabbergast Dulkinna into having a heart attack while watching the news on TV.

Dulkinna did not know at the time of the hatred that the news woman had for her. She simply watched in disbelief and could not even mutter a word. The events were taking place in Siria, a country in turmoil, where people did not want the Tsarina over-liminal.

Maddened by the fact that Dulkinna had shut herself down rather than have a heart attack, Judy decided to 'up the ante' and never take no for an answer until she killed Dulkinna, she destroyed Mikhail and killed every one of their children that she could.

CHAPTER THIRTY FOUR

Mr Kauffman And His Baleful Influence On The Game And The American Economy

Once in 2011 when returning from hiking with Ioobe, Dulkinna was almost hit by a convertible when walking to the parking lot. The driver, an exceptionally sexy young man, pulled into the parking lot, took a sip of water and waited patiently for the policeman to come and talk to him.

"This looks like somebody I know from back home" Dulkinna thought to herself. She was not at all phased by the incident, she was more preoccupied to figure out if she knew the man, or if he just reminded her of someone.

"A sexy young man, that is what you called me Dulkinna?"

"Sorry, I thought you look familiar."

"I ought to be!…I am from your hometown. We met years ago at a wedding. Remember the mathematics professor, Mr. Kauffman? I am his son…"

"Yes, she said excited, he was renowned in town for being one of the best math teachers, I met him once in eight grade…"

"Well, do not be so excited madam, he is the one who always flabbergasts you to not be able to remember even 7 times 6 without mnemonic devices. He does that just for fun. If we talk about him he will come on line…He is a jealous husband to be and he hates that you are as intelligent as you are…"

???…………………

"I will talk to you later madam, I am not myself, sorry about the incident, I had just returned from my wife's burial…"

"I am sorry to hear that…"

…………………………………………………………………………..

Later in the night, Dulkinna was awoken by the young Mr. Kauffman who needed someone to talk to.

"I am sorry, I know how you feel about people doing this sort of thing, but I feel so down on my luck…I need to talk to an old acquaintance…We met at a wedding reception years ago…I was the cousin of the bride…remember Nona? I am her cousin. We were seated near each other…'cute young man' that is what you told yourself then, I am glad to hear you did not change your opinion after all these years…"

"I am happy to feel you're smiling…"

"Yeah, my wife and I were not very close lately… It feels strange… she died suddenly of a heart attack…we were making love…She was Karina, do you remember Karina?…yes, you do, that Karina…"

Dulkinna did not need, nor could she say a word. The young man was in an agitated and sad mood and was inclined to talk about mutual acquaintances from their home town. He also was eager to introduce himself…as a husband to be…

Native of the same small town with the Tsarina, as she was to find out after a couple of long conversations, he had been invoked as a Tsarina killer by his family.

"I think though that this is a lot of BS, he said repeatedly. What matters is how you were raised and educated, not what your stupid parents wished for when you were conceived…"

He managed to peak Dulkinna's interest…They talked many nights about his departed wife, his father in law who had been the Tsarina's teacher, his father, the math teacher…what he was eager to talk about, was his admiration for the Tsarina's spirituality. He was in love with her books, he had been on line with her while she was writing and bought and read every one of them. He loved her poetry and asked her jokingly to write something for him.

Mr. Kauffman had a duality in himself, determined by the intervention of the Tsarina's grandmother, who wanted to avert the malefic intentions of the Kauffman family. A very strong woman at subliminal level, she had found out about the intentions of the family to invoke a son, killer of the Tsarina, so she was alert and when she heard their invocation she tried to fend for the curse on the head of the new child, by asking heavens to send:

"The one who will follow her everywhere like a puppy!"

"So, do not tell me that your grandmother was not a Queen of Sheba!"

"Being a strong person at subliminal level and having the power to invoke you to come from heaven and not from hell, is not synonymous with being a Queen of Sheba, Mr. Kauffman. My grandmother asked for you to come from heaven…your grandmother wanted a killer, remember?"

....

The two times she saw him, at over-liminal level, Dulkinna could only describe him as sexy. With boyish good looks and somewhat effeminate features, at 2m tall, Dulkinna's favorite feature in a man, he was quite charming at subliminal level as well, she found after many other subliminal level conversations...

He told her that he was one of the directors of the game, working for Michelle Clinton…he had been hired some five years ago and he was in charge of the main game put forth by Dulkinna's employer, a major bank…

Without too much scruple, he jumped from one subject to another, eager to get her to do things he wanted her to do, or to give her the stories and shows he had prepared for her game. Most of all, he was obsessed with being with her at subliminal level when she was making love to Ioobe and even when she was not. Even though he was of superior mind and abilities, he was one of those men who were crazed by the machine's capabilities. He loved giving her sexual desires and leaving her "want for his sex…" as he used to put it. He became one of those men, Dulkinna became fearful of, only to figure out, that they also had children together.

His maleficent character and intentions, coupled with the good looks, determined the Tsarina to propose that he might be an incarnation of Lucifer the most beautiful of angels, who got all of them thrown out of heaven. He was furious at the comparison…

Mr Kauffman was trained by the Romanian secret services and made to believe that he has to act as a husband to be, in order to gain the Tsarina's trust. He had mainly Jewish children with the Tsarina, which were terrorized and killed even before those coming from Ioobe, by the Romanian harpie, for pure experiment and sheer joy of killing. She used to pretend that the Jewish killed Jesus, so, now, in turn she should terrorize and kill the children coming from the Tsarina and her Jewish husband to be.

As the Tsarina soon figured out, Mr. Kauffman did not shy away from any shenanigan, but when on his own free will and best behavior, he tried to protect the children. Not only was he trying to shield the ones of his own blood, but he even helped Mikhail with his own children on numerous occasions…

He had a visceral hate for the Tsarina and her two husbands, which may have been stemming from his hatred for his own mother and the fate she had reserved for him, to be a 'fugitive in time', constantly trying to kill the Tsarina.

Due to his inclination to sometimes save the children and to his good looks, many people had been enamored with the young man, modeling themselves after him, trying to pretend to be him at subliminal level on line and even opted for raising his children rather than their own.

One of those enchanted by the young Kauffman, was the atheist.

A scientist, the atheist was 'chained' to a wheelchair and could only communicate at subliminal level and through the use of a computer with thought recognition. He wanted to show his rage and lack of reverence for God, every time he spoke to the Tsarina. He just could not suffer her religious fervor, coupled with her high intelligence. He used to explain to her that only the power of the mind matters and there can be no such thing as a celestial God.

"So where does the power of the mind come from?" asked Dulkinna.

"I do not know how to answer that."

"And if there is no God, who created the nature's intelligent laws, the laws of physics, chemistry even, where do they come from…"

"So you believe that the world was created 5000 years ago?"

"Of course not, but I believe it was created by God."

"But this is not what the scripture says."

"You have your spirituality and I have mine." Snapped Dulkinna. "I believe in the existence of God, I believe in Jesus Christ, I happen to believe that many passages of the Bible were written by humans…'erare humanum est'…"

"So you believe in the dinosaurs…"

"Yes, of course! I believe in the dinosaurs also…"

"how can you be so intelligent and believe in a celestial being!"

"OK, who created the dinosaurs and where did the Big Bang come from?…but most of all, where do all the intelligent laws of physics and chemistry come from, why and how can there be so much intelligence even before man? There was no human mind at the time, was there?…"

With the atheist, Dulkinna discussed the duality pervasive in Mr. Kauffman's behavior and while the atheist found him fascinating, Dulkinna was maintaining that by analyzing his behavior and that of Hillary Obama, one can demonstrates that God exists.

"Mr. Kauffman himself maintains that he had been summoned in a certain way and when observing his duality, I can only conclude that the devil is real. And if there is a devil, there must be God…"

"But your religion says that this is blasphemy…"

"Of course it is! But I am trying to use the logic, which is YOUR religion, is it not?…For me the existence of God is simple. Trying to demonstrate that He did not exist is blasphemy, as you know, from what I can see and He would only forsake the one who doubts His existence, so, the whole experiment would be flawed. The first commandment tells me: 'I am your God', while the second one tells: 'There is no other God but I"…so, for me, this is it. I do not need more proof."

"Why would you maintain that Mr. Kauffman is an evil man?"

"Well, I think evil is characterized by stupidity, envy and hatred. Mr. Kauffman is a jealous man and, due to his sheer blindness during his pangs of fury at myself and my husband, as you know, he becomes invariably a business imbecile. To me, that is the proof. He is cursed and it shows in his business endeavors. He was cursed by his mother and grandmother who invoked him and then raised him to be a killer. That is psychotic behavior. In my book, he is a sociopath. Remember his killing of my sister who fell in love with him…the one conceived by the Romanian harpie from my mother's eggs and the politician."

"I do, but I also remember him being the one who brought you back to life when you killed yourself…"

"By pretending to be Mikhail, I remember that also…but it was not him who brought me back to life, it was the Hindu doctor who started praying to 'the God of the Tsarina'. At least this is how Mr. Kauffman and Mr. Obama related the story to me…"

"He is the father of your beautiful daughters Camilla and La Vie…"

"He is also good friend with the hacker and, he helped create many of the terrorist systems and destroyed the game in later years, by condoning cheating in the game, by dilapidating funds and by personally destroying my health …

"We all did that Dulkinna…"

"What do you mean all? Please do not tell me this..!"

"I am a queen of Sheba, Dulkinna, I cannot believe in a God who would forsake us the way your God has forsaken me…"

Dulkinna remembered how Mr. Kauffman tries to overtake even his children, for whom he maintains to have loving feelings, during his trance periods.

She started eating. It was time to eat and go to sleep…

CHAPTER THIRTY FIVE

The Children Of America

The Perils Of The Young Generation.

Dulkinna had known little Viviana ever since the little girl was a couple of hours old. She had been the one to ask for 'a child with a good mind for learning' when pretending to play fairy godmother to the unborn child. Miss-interpreting Dulkinna's intentions, her friend felt offended and instantly said that 'she hoped not'. Dulkinna loved the children of all her friends, never missed the opportunity to shop for lots of kiddy presents, pretending that she was shopping for her own children and took an interest in the development of every one of them.

This Easter, she wanted especially to see little Viviana again. She liked the kid's spunk. She was supposed to be an old soul, as Mikhail read her and Dulkinna knew from subliminal level, that the mother was training the little girl to kill the Tsarina's children. That seemed impossible to be true, for a mother to train her little toddler to become a killer, yet, Dulkinna thought that even though it can always be the truth she should be courteous to the friend and the child. After all, she always had taken everything with a grain of salt.

Sure enough, she met little Viviana and her parents and was glad to run into them in the church's yard. Viviana was playing with her friend who was a year older. The little boy, wanted to find a snake to kill. They played for a couple of hours, a 'little gang' of toddlers, trying to find vermin to kill, literally. The father wanted to get her to talk to Dulkinna and Ioobe, but the toddler, even though smiling, was not interested at all. At the end of the day, when to say good bye, the voices at subliminal level started warning the Tsarina:

"no children, no more children, we cannot cope anymore, the children will try to kill you, please madam, no more children!"

"The children are too strong at subliminal level madam!"

It was hard to believe them. So, Dulkinna just wanted to say goodbye to Viviana and there it was, the confirmation. The kid was locked into trance, she had a transfixed look on her face and while the father, Ioobe and Dulkinna were all trying to 'wake her up', the mother had a smug about her and tried to hide her face from Dulkinna. In the end, Dulkinna and Ioobe left the church yard, while the child never gave up trying to kill them at subliminal level. A 3 year old child of a 'good' friend......................

Little Paris, was only 1 year old when the Tsarina met her and the proud parents. They exchanged business cards at church. Now, Paris is 7 and the voices at subliminal level constantly talk about the kid having killed a peer, in order to become more popular and in order to become strong at subliminal level. The child mother's Mary resolve to kill the Tsarina at all cost, again seemed untrue when using Dulkinna's reasoning and yet, the mother always goes on line and threatens to kill the Tsarina, while calling at over-liminal level and inviting her to come visit. No confirmation was noticed at over-liminal level, but at subliminal level, Dulkinna figured the voice of her 'friend',

The adolescents and their need to be cool, the daughter of the high-school friend that hated Dulkinna because she was supposedly an imbecile, her mother paid for destroying the Tsarina's health and the personal doctor who could not deal with the fact that his mother was not the Tsarina.

All these could have been coincidences, of sorts, or they could be confirmation for..: THE GAME.

The people wanted Dulkinna to stop eating, because they were gaining weight when they had already eaten and then Dulkinna started to eat. They felt the need to eat themselves, since they kept themselves at subliminal level connected to the machine.

The people wanted Dulkinna to eat more, because they were absolutely starving all the time. When eating at the same time and the same thing and quantity with the Tsarina, they were flabbergasting her. In other words, by pretending to 'be the Tsarina', or others 'with the Tsarina', they were closer to her. This is what the hacker and his wife were doing. So were many others. Dulkinna was eating very healthy food all the time and she tried to keep the calories below 1200 so as to not gain any extra weight if she were not fattened artificially. Because of this, the flabbergastors were starving.

The people wanted Dulkinna to eat more beef. In the game, this was the symbol for "them having some beef with…" and so they 'got the podium' to vent their grievances on line or to get others to listen to them and be programmed.

The people wanted Dulkinna to stop eating beef. It was offending the Hindu and it was against their own religion, if they happened to be Hindu, so that they could not become flabbergastors.

The people wanted Dulkinna to eat more chicken. It was low in calories and every religion could tolerate the behavior. Almost, as noted by the Dalai Lama.

The people wanted Dulkinna to stop eating chicken. In the game, this was the symbol for being a chicken and not having an opinion.

The people wanted Dulkinna to stop eating pork…..

DULKINA'S PORTFOLIO

Should we renew tante Aurora?

Time travel isn't supposed to be happening, right? Today we can renew ourselves; routinely we hear stories of people who are 116 years old and within a two hour surgical procedure they are transformed to look, feel and be 16 again.

The Machine has made that possible for us! The subject has become mundane, the process of creating a new body for the old brain with just a vile of blood and symbiotic liquid, is now a well established technology, with no glitches anymore

Should we do it without a doubt, or is this something we should ask society about?

If tante Aurora one day comes home looking like a kid, are we obligated to still love her? Should we accept her impositions and still consider her the elder, or should we decide that she is supposed to fight life again like the rest of us? Are the authorities: police, FBI, etc. Alone to give their permission or is her family and friends entitled to an explanation and request for an approval as well?

Sure, we are all entitled to reach the Mathusalemic age, but should our old support system be disrupted and shocked or should we decide together how and when to renew? What if she has the tendencies of a serial killer, what if she wants your life and that of the kids to suit her please and not yours or their own? Should we decide together on some boundaries, on how things are going to be done in the future and how much we can accept, how much we can not? Should she renew herself to be 16 again or 47, is it her saying alone? Should we venture our opinion, should it be asked, demanded or necessary? These questions will help us understand the 'threat' of the little old lady, or are they nearly never enough?

Dulkina writes an essay

"Overliminality! I am for people addressing frankly and directly the issues they are faced with in every day life. Without calling issues exactly for what they are, without my being allowed to answer my detractors, I could not continue in good conscience discussions at subliminal level. The words twisted, issues taken out of context and accusations to which I cannot answer, in forums to which I do not have access to, give rise to miscommunication and mistaken assumptions or wrong decisions.

I would probably hesitate less to give my opinion on the facts of the day, if I would have the right to answer my critics. More than that, I wish I had the control over what is being said in my name, where and by whom.

Without overliminality, a government can contend that corruption is a 'right' or 'freedom' of the politician, while the citizen has to 'pretend' that arguments against such outrageous behavior ought be really well thought off and thoroughly defended. This, because the people are forced to talk while making abstractions and using generalizations because the precise issues are sort of a taboo. One cannot use direct, straight talk as long as one has to pretend certain facts are true, others are supposed to be read in between the lines. Some people think they understood, while others laugh at the fact that the truth has not been told anyway, mockery becoming the only reality that one could count on! Violence seems without reason, when coming from a place inside a soul which cannot reconcile between the reality spoken and the one lived, any longer.

Protests against the government that decided to deride its own citizens, will come to be understood by some as a thing 'to live with', sort of a 'necessary evil', while, the protesters, misunderstood or mocked, inevitably become hysterical when their voices and efforts are not heard or seen. This can lead to a series of different consequences, all of which are bad for democracy and bad for the moral fiber of society.

Arguments for example, like 'we have been elected and now have a mandate to do whatever we consider to be right'.-seem to be difficult to fight against to some, but only on first thought. When analyzed more profoundly one cannot help to not realize the Gould claims are violently insolent, towards the psyche that expected his or her elected official to become part of a democratic mechanism of a civilized society.

Offensive language need not be employed, for the individual to consider that his dignity has been stepped upon and personal rights trespassed. Governing by decree, especially when such decree tenets go against the common sense, is not something a member of any society in the world today, is prepared to accept. Even under a totalitarian regime, a newly elected official, is expected to act and behave consistent with a common sense dictated logic. A 'revolution by decree' is impossible to accept as long as there is no consensus.

The Goulds want their Gould state.

The 'free people' want a revolution of the mind, body and spirit, the freedom to think, talk and act on ones own free will. Free from Goulds, masters of our own bodies and fate.

The first, is an affront to reason everywhere, while the later seems to be something many thought to have been self understood and available as a given. The hurting psyche is not something to be ignored for long. Neither that of the individual, nor that of society as a whole. Doing so, will bring the unwanted violence. Painful as it is, we find ourselves today, having to ask for the right to be on our own free will. Painful as it is, we find ourselves having to come out in the street to protest elected officials who want to highjack democracies, to ignore the tenets of 'civilization', even to decree from their newly acquired positions, that once they have been elected, they have a mandate to do as 'they consider'. The electors Do Not Even Have The Right to ignore such practice. It is our civic duty to protest in such a case. It is a duty towards ourselves, our children, our society and our democracy.

The Character

The character of this lady had been tested time and again. The higher-ups decided to send two other analysts with her to New York. Do they not trust her still? The novice in her asked introspectively.

They constantly tell her she is too shy. 'If by shy, you mean somebody who respects and demands boundaries when it comes to human interaction, guilty as charged-she always muttered to herself; But I am not afraid of you, buddy.'- she kept motivating herself at subconscious level.

There was such a feeling of unease that she was again repeatedly sighing and starring at her computer's keyboard, contemplating resignation. She knew full well that was not an option. Not with the mortgage on the house they loved so much having to be paid. Iubi had just passed the qualifier exam and was now working on the PhD thesis. No option of resigning any time soon, better drink a glass of wine and go to sleep. Tomorrow will be a better day?

The company was not even going to sponsor her green card application. She was still dependent on Iubi's visa as an international student's spouse. She had this job though: investments analyst. This is what she dreamed about during graduate school this was her dream job and they had just bought their dream house. All on her salary, while Iubi was still a student... things could not be better...? The parents and family back home, were enviously happy for the 'Americans'...Almost nowhere to turn to...for an honest talk about how stressful this job was.

The flight tomorrow is early in the morning...12am. The wine did not do the trick, chances were she would go to the airport tired, after a sleepless night, trying to look perky, jovial, ready to evaluate the new system; in New York...That is not so bad, to have the opportunity to go to the New York vendor...to see everybody in their own environment, maybe the 'courteous customer service' could give her something to write about in the report.

The political decision had been made. In the merger and acquisition agreement, the new system had been chosen as the one from the acquired company. Everybody knew it. The due diligence requirements imposed that an analysis be made and the 'best' system chosen. The old system was by far better, in her opinion. It was from a reputable Wall Street firm, with live feeds information and the customer service had been impeccable. This system that the acquired company had been using, is from a relatively new corporation, trying hard to make up in customer service relationships for what it lacked in terms of market information and reports available. Her two coworkers kept stressing this aspect and how thrilled they were with the customer service department... She was known to be a brainiac, always sticking to the technical aspects and arguments in every discussion. They left it to her to evaluate the reporting capabilities. Ha, Ha, Ha, the joke seemed to be on her again, not on them.. But as always, she had her sense of humor, working for her. She would evaluate all the pros and cons and allow the SVPs to decide which system was better.

She'd been told to 'get over herself', that she is too serious, that she needed to be 'less nice' etc. This one was the favorite of the entire headquarters, that she just needed to be 'less nice'. This she had to accept from people who smiled with no apparent reason, whenever they met another person, she used to smile inside, mocking the opponent.

She had been also accused of being to succinct. 'Now we can all go home' --one of the SVPs said after one of her presentations, -'she covered everything I need to do in my job'. She valued his opinion, so she made a mental note, that the report this time has to be more detailed in scope, but leave some issues to the judgement and decision of the high-er-ups. The CEO was always praising her work, so were her boss and everybody else, but she could not shed the feeling of stress, of constantly feeling judged, sometimes mocked, both loved and hated by her coworkers.

In the cafeteria, everybody wanted to join her. The conversations inevitably used to converge towards 'How do you do this or that in the old country?' so, she constantly made mental notes that she has be become more 'American' -- now that she nailed down smiling without any particular reason whatsoever.

They were not so bad and this is a dream job for every American, she had been so lucky to land it write after graduation, that she practically did not dare complaining even to mother on the phone. The work hours were sometimes 10, sometimes 12 hours a day, but it was not bothering her that much. She returned to a beautiful home and a loving husband...and there were no children to worry about.

And yet, she felt popular. She was the one all came to before their own meetings, to ask her technical questions, knowing that she loved to go out of her way to help anybody. 'Why do you do this all the time?'-she had been asked...The answer inevitably came 'just doing my job, you *know...' -- smiling, of course and noting to herself, to learn everything about this company, what do you think buddy, I just deliberately do not have a life for no reason?*

Did it happen for her husband to call, mentioning dinner was almost ready, for her to tell him she was going to be home soon and then to receive a request for a report to be ready by 8 am in the morning? Yes...many times, but Americans are known for their efficiency, for their time is money attitude, so she wanted to become just like the best of them. 'Never say no' was actually advice from the accounting executive one time. 'So, how will you figure out when I disagree She asked.'

Reports slicing the information in each and every way possible, modeling new assets, financial engineering done 'yesterday' on a new product, these were the everyday duties of the analytics department and she loved that she was in the center of it all. She knew almost everybody in the entire headquarters and everybody knew her. 'pick me, pick me'- she once mocked herself, while asking an executive to allow her to work for him on a 'just another thankless tasks'.It took its toll though. This was not the first time, starring at the computer keyboard, late in the day, crying on the inside, contemplating resignation and one day starting to work for herself."

It Was Fate

I was born in 1965 in a town in the middle of the Romanian Moldova, called Bacau. I was the first born of Adina and Lony. They say I really was the most beautiful new born they have ever seen, no kidding or fibbing...I came after about 12 hours of labor, my mother says and I had the most perfect skin for a new born. I believe it. After all, why not? Somewhere, someone, is supposed to have had the most beautiful baby ever born, why not my mom?

At the time, my parents who had been living with my maternal grandparents obtained their first two bedroom apartment and furnished it accordingly, for the new princess. As a baby, I was fitted with white, red and pink diapers, as a toddler, the little dresses started to come from the fashion houses in Bucharest. I feel only now, that I was being spoiled. Then, I just did not accept anything black or too dark in color. My grandmother to me was like a mother and my mother, almost like a big sister. I called her Liliuca.

In the summer of '69 my little paradise was about to start changing. Liliuca was pregnant with her second child, a boy, they were going to call Linu, who was born a little before my fourth birthday...And they brought him home... Now, when I hear the song of Bryan Adams, I relate to it, as if it really was the best time of MY life, since I have a lot of memories on my grandma's porch, carefree, playing, sometimes butt naked, near a baby stroller, where a chubby little bundle was sleeping.

On one of those days, my dad received the word that he had to go on a business trip to Bucharest. Well, he had to drag along the naughty 'elder one', as I was suddenly called, because the little one was a hand full. He said yes. And so, I was informed, that daddy is going to Bucharest, to buy me some new things and I get to go with him and we were going to fly for the first time in my life. Oh, joy!

"Your ears might hurt from flying though, what do you think?"
"No, not MY ears!"
"Are you sure?"
"Yes, I will open my mouth and show you my tongue, like grandma told me and they will not hurt!"
"All right"

They forgot to mention the big noise of the engine!...We caught the next flight and off we were.

In the Bucharest airport, there was a man selling Helium filled balloons in shapes of different animals. OH, joy! They were expensive, but I really liked a dragon looking one, in a greenish color. In the evening, when my dad came from his meetings, we played with the balloon, which was flying in the room, close to the ceiling and I, was jumping up and down the table, pretending that I fly with my dragon. My aunt was studying in Bucharest and was living in the apartment of her brother, a football star. She hosted us for the couple of days and was going to the University in the morning, my dad to the company he was supposed to be visiting and I...alone in the apartment for a couple of hours. I was a good kid, don't worry. I always did almost what I was told...

On one day, I got out on the balcony and...while watching some kids play outside, supervised by their grandmother, I pushed my head between the rails of the balcony and...it fit! Trying to pull back,...not so much! So, the old lady, pushed her chair underneath my balcony and started entertaining me...At least I was not crying...After about an hour, my dad came home, pushed and then pulled me gently back inside and promised that the next day, he will take me to the park, if I promise to not be scared or have nightmares about what happened. It worked like a charm.

The next day, off to the park, me with my flying dragon tied nicely to my index finger. I really do remember people turning their heads. Some for the expensive and rare dragon balloon, some admired the dress I wore, some, were just pretending that I was really pretty. A lady approached us with a little boy about my age, who said:

"I want her to give me her dragon!"

And I did...???

"Really, Dulkina, your dragon? can he take it home with him?"
"Yes"-short answer.
"Maybe they are meant to be! they should marry some day," the lady said to my dad...

Well, I think you guessed: Years later, I went to the University in Bucharest and I met a boy, about a year older, born in the year of the dragon, who started following me around and doing everything I wanted. Flowers in hand every day, he was smart and smart looking. We graduated the same college and one day, I told him the story of the dragon...

He looked up to me and said:
"That was aunt Violet and...I AM THE ONE!"....."

If I were the presidente

Dulkina was working on her new assignment. She found it difficult.... It had to go to print in two days and it involved the writing of an article starting with the phrase: If I were the Presidente.

If I ever would have considered to run for public office, it would only be to become Presidente. I think it is the only office that could help me literally change the world. There are scores of public servants who could do their part, they really are trying hard to do their part, but without clear and strong leadership, their voices are lost in the white noise of those branded as naïve or even liars.

Take for example the issue of fighting for a green planet. Every public company out there, trying to bring us solar power, or hydroelectricity from the ocean's waters, or even wind energy, is doing its own part. But together, they will achieve little nothing without the strong encouragement and clear vision from the White House or even from a No. 10 Downing Street, etc. The strategy of achieving a green planet, has to have a good master plan, at global level and the American presidency needs do its part. If I were the Presidente, I would fight for that. An even more dear issue to my heart, the writer of this article, is freedom of the mind, body and spirit. With the advent of the Big Thought Reading Machine, we have achieved technologically the un-immaginable. Our minds can now be read, the very process of thought formation can be known to the Big Thought Reading Machine, faster than we, ourselves, can become aware of it. Laws for behavior at subliminal level, are now an absolute must and the people who want to maintain control of their own mind, body and spirit, every creative mind, every breathing soul, let us dub them 'the free people' have a duty toward themselves. This duty is to make sure that they have sparred no effort, to ensure that they are indeed the owners of their own creative mind, that their actions are not dictated by a Goauld via the Big Thought Reading Machine, or even through the power of the Goauld's mind. If I were Presidente, I would fight for this.

The employment of the Hexagon Network via a Foundation that would prevent the government from abusing too high a power that it now has over its own countrymen and women would create the opportunity to protect every citizen at subliminal level, from Goauld intrusion. Creative minds have to be protected both from outside and inside intruders. Would be spies as well as other wrong doers have to be deterred not only by the new laws of behavior at subliminal levels. The Hexagon Foundation would be potentially brought to questioning both by the Government, Corporations and the Free People individually. A system of checks and balances would be created. As it is now, with the secret services and military holding the Hexagon, the government's power is too dangerously big over its own people. If I were Presidente, I would fight for this.

Raising the standard of living, even in the advanced nations such as America, via increasing the purchasing power of the lower middle class and eradicating poverty is another subject, that our dear officials consider as 'naive'. In a decade when there are negative interest rates for bank deposits, due to the fact that there are huge quantities of cash amassed by corporations and a lack of purchasing power by the masses, this project could and must be tackled. If I were Presidente, I would fight for this.

Taxation has reached levels for which increases are hard to bear, while. the external debt figures reached astronomical proportions. It is impossible to figure how our children would be able to pay this debt which is now larger than the annual GDP, without some creative solutions from Corporate America. The barriers of entry for new comers seem to have gotten too high, while established monster corporations do not bear their load. Fighting to 'make the pie bigger' rather than constantly have a 'run for food' and calls for class fighting, is one of the most important macro-economical policy calls for change, that can actually work. If I were Presidente, I would fight for this.

The recent scandal, of public corporations having diverted billions of dollars into Goauld pockets on account that their cash reserves were too large and management and politicians wanted them to become again 'mean and lean', is outrageous. The fact that there were too large cash reserves, is true. That only means though, that maybe we would now find the time and willingness to look into improving the security of future retirees, by bringing back the idea of defered consumption for some of these funds. Find a way to solve the problems with the Social Security in these times of huge cash deposits, would be a good idea. If I were Presidente, I would fight for this.

Raising the level of education before superior education, to levels appropriate for a country who wants to maintain competitive advantage and leadership in cutting edge technologies, is mandatory. We do have, I think, the best system for superior education in America, today. However, the profficiency level of those who are obligated to stop at a High School diploma, is not up to par within the world's rankings. Education can never fall of the agenda of any American President. If I were Presidente, I would fight for this. Do not look for my, Dulkina's name on the ballot. You will never find it. Instead, look for a candidate who is not affraid to dream big for his country and countrymen. A candidate, who would have the gaul to challenge the status quo, to talk thaugh and not be affraid he would be made a fool of. The trick is, he should really know how not to allow himself to be made a fool of. There will be detractors and bullies and maybe a bully is what we need for ourselves sometimes, in turn. I am not a bully, but if I were Presidente, I would find a way...

I would find a way to tell the lobbyists, the legislators and the cabinet members: Fight for America until your last drop of sweat. Fight to give the creative minds of this country a fair chance. Remember that 'pursuit of happiness' and do not be naive to consider that the mere mentioning guarantees it. We have to fight for it in every election, every campaign trail and every single day. If you do not reject the Goauld way of living, with a handful of people, virtually enslaving the creative minds of the multitudes, you cannot speak of every citizen's right to the pursuit of happiness any more. When some are allowed to consider themselves above the law, even if just a few, all others have lost their claim to blind justice and fair treatment under the legal system."

Cancer is now cured overnight

"Dulkina never blinked.

"Yes, the article will be about the power to cure all cancer forms overnight."

"Are you sure, you are not even overliminal yet?"

"The sooner people know, the better!"

"But you cannot cure all these cancers..."

"I cannot cure them myself all of them, but Miruna and the Healer can and all of them use the power of the human mind and the Big Thought Reading Machine!"

"How did you stumble upon this?"

"While relaxing in the pool I think."

"Really?"

"What was the first form of cancer you ever cured?"

"I think the brain tumors given to me by the evil doers"

"What did you cure that with?"

"They told me that I have it, but I pretended that it is not true and went to sleep, like my grandmother had taught me a long time ago...I made a mental note that I will wake up healthy and refreshed...and I did. When I woke up, the system people told me that the tumor had been healed while I slept!"

"But then, you were not in the pool, were you?" "It was a little more complicated than this. I was in the pool and I heard the faintly voice of Vladimir Putin calling me and telling me to understand that he had been poisoned and will be dead soon..." I reacted incredulously at first by denying that it was the truth but when he instead, I called upon the Healer and Miruna and told them: "Remember when I detoxified myself with olive oil and grapefruit juice and had all that elimination of toxins, how about you go back in time on the system, create a snapshot of my system then and then connect Vladimir to that 'baby bottle' so that he has the same kind of elimination and tell him at subliminal level to heal himself and rid of all toxin from his body. Tell me if you could obtain it!"

"The 'baby bottle' you called it?"

"Yes, this would render his system clean as that of a baby!"

"Done!"

"What do you mean?.."

"I have it," said Miruna.

"Put him on it and tell the Healer to continuously talk to him on the machine about what I said."

"He started elimination, mother!;" The Healer said.

"What do you mean?"

"He is on the toilet and he does eliminate almost like you...those pea like liver stones...."

"seriously?"

"Yes, mom, seriously!"..

"We call this a 'baby bottle'?"

"Call it the 'detox bottle from Dulkina'"

"Oh, mom, that feels so goo..od..what are you doing now?"

"I am stretching in the water..."

"Oh, it feels good mom!"

"Create a 'bottle' and give to Vladimir. This one, you label as the 'relaxation bottle from Dulkina'"

"This is how I started creating the 'botles'.

"How many bottles do they have now?"

"I do not know exactly, but Miruna became a specialist at creating and administering them with the help with the Big Thought Reading Machine."

"We now, have bottles for almost any affliction that people learned to cure or survive, that we learned of." -they heard Miruna talking, on the system.

"In this day and age, 2016, cancer has become a curable disease! If one has the machine and needs any kind of cure, one can now simply call on the system and they can connect you with the needed and appropriate 'bottle' if there is one for the affliction, or, the Healer together with the system people and the machine, can help you heal yourself, with the power of your own mind, amplified by the Big Thought Reading Machine and the system people."

"Some of the cancers I have cured in myself, Dulkina wrote, are the intestinal cancer and the brain tumor. I keep in check liver and kidney cancer. I also have a bottle for brain aneurisms, which can be cured with the power of the machine, as well."

"How dare you write such things, bitch? You are the anchor and it is not for you to advertise to people what are the powers of the Big Thought Reading Machine!"

The haters were all over it, as usual.

She went on to write about the health avatar and the cursed and security avatar that she had described in the previous discussions on the line. She described how it is now possible to create an accurate depiction of your system, call it the health avatar and how your doctor would work first with the avatar to maximize the healing potential and minimize side-effects if any and then, would place the avatar in contact with you, so that you can take your prescription if any and with and under the care of the bottles, cure yourself, with minimum side-effects. The benefits of the machine working with Dulkina's DNA did not stop here. It was now possible to have esthetic surgeries they said to her, that would replace ones skin with younger looking skin printed and build from said person's own DNA.

"What are you promising? Eternal youth?"
"They are, not me, I just found out about it from the line."
"We already have done this!", came the comment from the system people.
"Do not give it to her! She cannot have that surgery! We spent so much time destroying her body and her skin and for what?" - The Goulds shouting on the line were hysterical again.

"We hate her with her 7000 I.Q. and her being the anchor of the machine...why not one of us?"
"She is too intelligent!"
"Kill her!"
She smiled and continued writing on her article...."

Evil in the government

"When the government decides to demolish the individual, nothing else is left for anybody to build on. The communist era has shown us how a society can be destroyed, its people humiliated and demolished, how the economy itself would self-destruct. This whole fiasco was due to the government and society's concerted participation in the destruction of the individual.

The dissecting of the individual's psyche even, in order to put it back together again and again with its DNA slightly changed, with the wish to have our soul reengineered and 'adapted' so that when needed, it will answer to the government's call for submissive, docile response. With no regard for personal freedom, no right to consider any options out, just submissive, docile agreement to co-exist. To have such practice come to free societies would be absolutely the last stop before Judgment Day. It would really be akin to ending the world. When the individuals are led to believe that they are 'free' to consider options, yet the only one available is again, submission to government's will, the damage produced is so pervasive, so profound that it cannot be comparable to any other self destructing societal behavior.

Setting up the individuals for failure, for personal attacks to their own core belief, in order to obtain the slightest of approvals and applauding choruses of individuals agreeing en masse to accept attacks to their own personal self interests. This would be the ultimate in government evil. Pretending to care, in order to just mask a fear of commitment to the needs of society and demolishing the individual so that it does not even realize what his or her needs are, through a perpetual reminder that basic needs have changed and the 'need' for luxuries, frills or secured, self accomplished goals is futile. In turn, the perpetual stress and fears of not having met the minimum requirements on our to do lists, took their place.

Never comfortable, always under the impression that the impending gloom is a personal fault and that it should even be hidden from friends and family, leaving us no choices, but some sort of a suicide of the soul, which is never cared for, never gets to take its own turn on our priority list. The worst prostitution of all, when we sell it to the devil and then do not even look back, pretending it never happened, that we had no choice, that we simply needed to 'conform'.

Our body becomes a burden, that we carry around in order to satisfy a sexual need for finding a better US, an individual that we'd be more proud of, or even a better fit for the 'mechanism' of society. We forget how to restore it, we do not have time for such un-cool behavior. Instead, we sleep and close our eyes on a deeper level, when our conscience is indeed attacked and destroyed, our soul tired just gives in and we inattentively go dormant."

Dulkinna looked at the clock, it was late at night. It was like awakening from a dream. The article she was writing on What If the Evil in the Government were absconded, was coming along fine. She started to converse with some of the people of the system at the subliminal level about what the article she just wrote was all about. About her worries that her children would be 'used and abused" as they were so many times. A mother's worries never fade away, never disappear are never forgotten. When everybody can read your mind with the Big Thought Reading Machine, this is the last thing you wish to think of. What if enemies were on the line? What if anybody will try to hurt her again?.....

-Do not worry madam, we are all here, nobody will hurt the kids.... or you. Now, heal that cancer of yours will you? The voices of the people of the system spoke to her.

She had forgotten about that, they had given her cancer again, to see if she can cure herself again. She did not wish to heal it anymore, but the thought of the children.....they still needed her.

The system people were chatting about her and her worries.....

-Just heal yourself, will you? ...."

EPILOGUE

There had been a time when every day, before the 'explosion' threat was over, the game was about Dulkinna going over-liminal. Lately, the network was organized the way Dulkinna envisioned, yet some petty business people were afraid their 'trade secrets would go out' and in America, at least, the network 'broke rank' since it was too difficult to keep track of so many things.

"Much easier to pretend and to lie to ourselves, it happens to the best of us.." she thought to herself.

Everybody was contending that either they 'do not want her' without even themselves, most of the time knowing what the heck they meant to say…or that they just do not know how to bring things to over-liminality.

Dulkinna was convinced that she lived in the real world, knowing the consequences of both her and their actions, while everybody else, seemed to want to live in a virtual reality world, were they thought that if they pretend to not give 'her' the confirmation, as the Romanian harpie used to say, nothing was wrong with their life.

A close acquaintance who had killed a friend with a hatchet, in order to become stronger at subliminal level, bank tellers who 'pretended' that their conversations had taken place at subliminal level (and not over the phone), an editor, who pretended a contract for a published book was 'subliminal' ergo not funneling the money to the author, was not embezzlement, these were things Dulkinna would have liked to write about in her novel, but did not want to. Because…she just could not pretend….

In her moments of despair, Dulkinna would pretend that the game was just for entertainment and that Mikhail was probably just 'handling' her, but that never lasted more than half a second. Either the hackers reacted, or Mikhail or one of the children, would ask her why would she do that? She invariably answered only at under-liminal and subliminal level. At over-liminal level, it seemed to her that she had the right, from time to time to feel miffed at a question like that, or maybe just overwhelmed, to say the least. But at subliminal level, the one where we, humans cannot help from telling the truth, the answer was, that these events were not in her plans, that meant she felt overwhelmed, used but worst of all, powerless. By pretending that things are not as serious, that she is just the butt of all jokes, she simply could deal for a couple of seconds with what was going on. She seemed more in control, to accept their disdain, as a matter of fact and pretend nothing else can come out of it.

Invariably, though, she had to admit that it was true. Even though they had lied so…almost all the time to her, Viviana did try to kill her on Easter, she did fatten 6 lbs in one day, from eating less than 1000 calories, she was flabbergasted to feel that her tooth needed a root canal and after the threat of explosion disappeared, everybody lost interest in doing that. Denying the existence of the children seemed almost a sin in her mind, at this point and then, it meant, things have indeed deteriorated more than humanly bearable in the last two years. So, as in previous years, she had conversations with the Dalai Lama, angered at the fact that he was 'being a spectator' at her enslavement, now, when she felt that the whole world was falling apart, she would address God directly, telling him that if it were not for His plan…..and the big cross she had to carry…her wishes would have been pretty simple, she always wanted just for a simple, honest life.

What Should My Life Have Been

If it were not for You,
I would have liked, oh God,
Three children to have had!

If it were not for You,
I would have liked, oh God,
My brother's wife to call my sister!

If it were not for You,
I would have liked, oh God,
My brother's children to have loved as my own!

If it were not for You,
I would have liked, my God,
My husband to love and obey!

If it were not for You,
I would have liked, my God,
The world to believe it were Your Kingdom!

If it were not for You,
I would have liked, my God,
I would have thought I knew my own name!

Please, Heavenly Father,
Let me know, what did You want me to say?
How should I ever begin to call Your name?

Am I to Your liking, am I the one that they say?
Or am I the one that I pretended to be?
Just a silly woman, who never knew how to pretend,
To have known what to say?

Was I supposed my body to think precious?
Was I supposed my health to wish for,
And try to keep whole?

Was I supposed to believe in You?
Or was I just to be the fallen Angel?

Because, God All Mighty,
They keep telling me,
That I might come from Thee!

Yours truly,
Dulkinna
(by the way, they keep calling me: "The Tsarina")

She wrote the poem on her Ipad, ate and went to sleep…

Printed in the United States
By Bookmasters